Spirited Shenanigans

CADAVER LAB

CAT JOHNSON

Chapter One

As a more or less private person, there were only certain things Natalie Chase was more than willing to confess aloud to others.

Telling Harper, Red and Bethany last year that she'd thought the new doctor in town was hot, in spite of the rumors that Liam might or might not be a serial killer? Easy. (The margaritas she'd consumed at the Muddy River Inn might have spurred on that confession.)

Admitting to Harper last year that she was overwhelmed with the workload at her new book and wine shop and needed help? Also (moderately) easy—and necessary.

Then there were things Natalie was dead set against revealing even to her closest friends.

That she'd been seeing—hearing, talking to, socializing with—ghosts since being electrocuted and technically dead for three and a half minutes last year?

That was *not* so easy.

In fact, as Harper and her fiancé Stone stood in front of Natalie waiting for the announcement she'd promised when she'd summoned them to Liam's lab, there were any number of unpleasant things she would far rather do than admit her secret.

She'd happily run naked down the village's Main Street instead of making this confession—even though she made sure all the light bulbs were low wattage in her apartment so Liam never got a really clear view of her sun-and-exercise deprived body.

She'd rather be locked in the spooky abandoned nursing home down the road—even though she knew it would be teeming with spirits.

But telling Harper and Stone that she'd been communing with the dead and lying about it to everyone except for Liam for over a year? That was the *dead* last thing on her list of unpleasant things to do— no pun intended.

Yet she'd succumbed to the pressure of others. Had let her supposed friend Gabe convince her to text Harper.

Why she'd let him have a say in what she did she

didn't know. He was a ghost. It wasn't like he was unbiased in the matter. Or could understand her plight as a living breathing human being.

It didn't matter that he'd been murdered. Cut off in the prime of his life. She could still hold him accountable for pressuring her into doing something she didn't want to do. Something she knew in her heart was a bad idea. Bad for her and bad for the spirit community of Mudville.

Peer pressure was real—even if it was a spirit doing the pressuring.

But as the local ghosts' human representative, wasn't it up to her to protect them from the many and sordid ramifications of exposure?

Yes. Yes, it was!

Natalie had a flash of what could happen to Mudville should the word get out.

She imagined hordes of spectators crowding the streets hoping for a ghostly encounter. Trespassing on private property. Wrecking the local farmers' fields with their RVs and all-terrain vehicles.

And the press! They'd be relentless once they learned.

She'd have no peace. She wouldn't be able to run her store. They'd block the entrances with their crews and news vans. Customers wouldn't be able to get in to shop.

With horror she remembered the disastrous live interview she'd done with Lucy Sunshine for WBNG News right after she'd been electrocuted and lived to tell about it. It had proved she was not a natural on camera.

Nope. That was an experience she never wanted to repeat. Not in this lifetime and—now that she knew about the existence of the spirit world—not in the afterlife either.

Harper was a good friend. But she was also a writer. She lived her life in a public way Natalie couldn't comprehend. Harper put everything about her own life, this town, and the people in it online for the world at large to see.

Yes, Harper's social media obsession had helped the shop enormously—saved it really—back in the early days when Natalie had been struggling to make a go of the new business.

Natalie was undyingly grateful for all of Harper's help and hard work, as well as her friendship.

Once Upon a Vine Books and Wine might not exist today without Harper. But Natalie couldn't trust her to keep a secret this big. Which left her with a decision. What was she going to tell Harper now instead of the truth?

She was going to have to wing it. Come up with some sort of confession on the fly. Something that wouldn't make it seem odd that she'd had both of them to come to Liam's lab.

As her friend stood expectantly waiting, Natalie began, "Harper, I have something to tell you."

While she paused to notice that she didn't have enough air in her lungs—she seemed to have forgotten how to breathe—Natalie heard Gabe gasp.

Invisible to Liam, Harper and Stone, Gabe turned to his equally invisible girlfriend next to him. "Millie, this is it. Nat's actually going to admit to another living she can see us."

She wanted to shush him. Snipe at Gabe to be quiet. Tell him that she had to think.

But she couldn't do any of those things without revealing her secret. And wasn't the point right now—her main goal—to hide that she could hear Gabe?

Blocking out the distraction—the constant ghost chatter that had been the soundtrack of her life for over a year—Natalie finally focused her mind. And thankfully, her mind delivered the perfect solution.

Fingers crossed that it would work, she sucked in a

big breath and let out on a whoosh of air, "Madame Letisha is a fraud."

Stone laughed. A sardonic sound ripe with sarcasm. "What? Natalie, are you saying that the ghost medium Harper hired. The lunatic who waved burning herbs around our house, spoke some mumbo-jumbo and then handed my fiancée a bill for a no-doubt outrageous amount she still won't admit to, is a fake? No. Say it isn't so."

As Stone rolled his eyes, a tight-lipped Harper shot him a sideways glance before focusing back on Natalie.

Meanwhile, Natalie was trying to ignore the judgmental rise of Liam's eyebrows as well as Gabe's scowl.

Millie however, having been raised as a proper Victorian lady by her mother, maintained a passive expression. Natalie thought she would have liked living during that era. It seemed so much more civilized— Millie's murder and subsequent dismemberment aside, of course.

"How do you know she's a fake?" Harper asked.

Good question. How could Natalie know except for the fact that she could actually see and talk to ghosts while the charlatan medium Harper had found on Google clearly could not?

Again, she wracked her brain for an answer.

The solution literally surrounded her. Liam's lab.

Liam was a scientist. He had equipment and stuff. He'd even brought some of it over to Harper's. That was it!

"Because Liam's machine picked up something *after* the house cleansing," Natalie blurted.

"It did?" Harper asked on a gasp.

Liam's dark brow cocked impossibly higher. So high he might as well have spoken aloud. Natalie imagined his words would have had a few cusses in them over her fib now involving him.

Harper spun to him now. "Liam, what did you catch?"

Liam turned his gaze pointedly away from Harper and said, "Natalie, why don't you explain? You're so much better at this than I am."

At that Gabe snorted. They all, the ghosts included, considered Natalie a shitty liar. But she'd been living this lie so far just fine.

Pretty much.

Mostly, anyway—

It was Gabe's fault Harper had heard him and Millie in her house which had spurred her to hire Madame Letisha—fraud though she was—to cleanse the house. And it was Gabe's fault Stone had heard him and Millie in the garden today.

His fault. Not Natalie's.

She'd have to remind him of that. Later.

Right now, she had some fibbing to do. They'd see. She'd pull this off too.

"Liam's recorder caught ghost voices after Madame Letisha claimed she'd cleared the house. The voice clearly said that Letisha was full of bullshit, but the ghosts would willingly leave the house out of respect for you."

Harper's eyes widened. "Oh, my God. *That* was on the recording?"

"Yes." Natalie nodded with pride over her very believable lie.

Ha! There. That should do it. Problem solved. Who was a bad liar now?

"Can I hear it?" Harper asked, looking excitedly at Liam.

Uh, oh.

"Um..." Natalie hadn't thought that far ahead and she seemed to be fresh out of lies.

"I sent it off to one of my researcher friends to see what he could make of it," Liam supplied smoothly.

She should be grateful he'd come to the rescue so quickly with that amazing excuse. But as his girlfriend,

Natalie considered it more than a bit disturbing just how smoothly Liam had lied.

"Didn't you keep a copy?" Harper asked.

"Didn't even think of it. Just sent the whole machine right off." Liam lifted one shoulder.

Damn, he really was good at this. But as Harper still studied them both too closely as she digested this tall tale, Natalie decided she'd better elaborate.

"He—the researcher—wanted to inspect the device as well as the recording," Natalie jumped in, picking up where he'd left off in the tag team lying. "But I thought you should know."

"Why didn't you tell me right away?" Harper frowned.

"*Before* she paid her," Stone added grumpily.

When Natalie froze like a deer in headlights, Liam jumped in again. "I was so busy I didn't listen to the recording until days later."

"Yup. Days and days. Almost a week really," Natalie added.

"But why didn't you tell me then?" Harper asked.

Crap, Harper asked a lot of questions.

"Well...you seemed so happy the disturbances had stopped. I didn't see the point. It was done. I thought it best to let it go. In fact, I only brought it up now because you were talking about hiring Madame Letisha for me. To clear the bookshop and the garden. So of course I had to say something—"

Liam squeezed Natalie's arm to quell her babbling and said, "We're really sorry. We should have told you."

Harper let out a breath. "No. I understand why you didn't. But oh, my God, I have to hear that recording. When can you get it back?" she asked Liam.

After a sideways glance at Natalie that conveyed his displeasure with this whole situation, Liam said to Harper, "I'll call my friend and find out. I'll let you know."

"Great. Thank you." Excited now, Harper spun to Stone. "We have to go. My head is swimming. I have to get it all down before I forget."

Stone drew in a breath. "You're going to write a book with ghosts in it now, aren't you?"

"You bet your sweet ass I am." Harper grinned, reaching for Natalie to envelop her in a hug. "Thank you, thank you, thank you. Both of you, for telling me. I'm so excited."

Oh, boy. What had she done?

Natalie forced a smile. "I see that. Now go, before you forget all your great ideas."

"I will. Thanks." Harper grabbed Stone's hand and as he said a quick goodbye, she dragged him out of the lab.

When the door slammed shut behind them, Liam crossed his arms over his chest and glowered at Natalie. "What now, Einstein?"

Ha! She'd already thought of that.

"We make an actual recording. Gabe says what I told Harper he said. We say Liam had the recorder in his pocket and turned it on in the attic after everyone else went downstairs so that's why only Gabe's voice is on it." When Gabe looked skeptical, Natalie added, "Stop. It'll work. She's so excited she won't question it."

Gabe, holding Millie's hand, shook his head. "You were going to tell her the truth. Nat, what happened?"

"Yes, Nat, what did happen?" Liam asked pinning her with his stare.

God how she hated the two men could gang up on her now. All because Gabe and Millie's love was so powerful that when the two ghosts touched they could, somehow, be heard by others and not just Natalie.

The power of love...

Wait. That was exactly what she needed right now. Love. It was just the thing to get her out of this sticky situation.

She narrowed her eyes at Liam. "If you really loved me, you'd understand."

With that she spun on her heel and stomped toward the door as she heard Gabe say, "Oh, man. You're in trouble now."

And Liam's grumbled, "Shit."

Natalie smiled. The power of love. It could also be used as a weapon.

Chapter Two

"Oh, my God," Harper gasped, not for the first time. She pressed a hand to her chest and repeated, "Oh. My. God."

"Jeez, somebody get this woman a thesaurus," Gabe mumbled. "I thought she was supposed to be a writer."

He turned and glanced at Millie, who did a half nod, half shrug of confirmation.

Meanwhile, unaware of the ghostly critics in the room, Harper hit the button to stop the recording from playing and spun to look wide eyed at Natalie. "Oh, my God."

At this, Gabe ran his hand over his face and Millie let out a little giggle from behind her fingers.

"This is real," Harper said rather than asked, sounding breathless with wonder.

"It is." Natalie nodded, happy to be telling the complete truth for a change.

"And you believe it—the voice—is an actual spirit?"

"One hundred percent, I do, " Natalie confirmed, once again, one hundred percent truthfully.

"And Liam recorded this in my bedroom in the attic?" Harper asked.

Oh, well. So much for being truthful...

"Yes," Natalie lied with a definitive nod she hoped made her answer seem extra convincing.

Harper spun to look at her fiancé. "Can you believe it?"

Stone had remained suspiciously silent up until now, although he did look a bit pale beneath his farmer's tan. "I don't *want* to believe it, Harper. We sleep in that room. We... do other things in that room. And there was a ghost watching us?"

Poor Stone. But she did share his horror over the reality of ghostly voyeurism. A shiver ran down her spine.

Swallowing hard, Stone glanced at Natalie. "Where is Liam, anyway?"

She couldn't admit that even though he had

showed her how to use the recorder so she could capture Gabe's voice in his lab earlier that day, Liam had refused to be there when she delivered the bogus recording to Harper and Stone.

"Uh, he had something important to do. A... meeting. A, uh, Zoom call actually. For his research." There. That sounded real.

More details always helped sell the lie. And Liam probably was working on his research project, which was something very important. So really, it wasn't all that much of a lie at all.

Stone-faced—no pun intended—Stone continued, "It's the same voice I heard in the garden."

He looked between her and Harper. And looked like he needed a drink.

"Which proves he—the ghost—did move out of the house. Just like he promised he would. He's in the garden now. See?" Harper was obviously in caretaker mode, trying to calm Stone. "At least he sounds like a nice ghost."

Harper reached out and squeezed Stone's hand, uncharacteristically assuming the role of the calm reasonable one in their relationship while Stone visibly freaked out.

If Natalie had to guess, Harper was worried he'd refuse to sleep in the house anymore. Since they were supposed to live there in her great aunt Agnes's house even after they got married, that could pose a problem.

"I'm nice *and* I'm handsome too," Gabe joked with a wink at Millie.

Luckily he hadn't been holding Millie's hand while speaking. Without the two entities having physical contact, Harper and Stone couldn't hear them speak. Only Natalie could. Why that happened, no one knew for sure. Gabe and the rest of the ghosts didn't get an instruction manual upon dying.

But not revealing themselves now was a smart move on Gabe's part. Hearing the tape had been enough of a revelation for Harper and Stone for one day. They didn't need to know they were in the midst of an up close and in person spiritual—or at least *spirit* —encounter here and now.

Harper spun back to Natalie. "But now that we have concrete irrefutable proof, we have someone else —besides the ghost—who we need to deal with."

"Who?" Natalie asked.

"That phony Madame Letisha." Harper scowled.

Uh oh.

"Uh, proof for what?" Natalie asked, fearing the answer.

"Proof to discredit her. We have to stop her from misleading other unsuspecting clients."

Shit. Was what had begun as a little white lie going to end up starting a war between Harper and Madame Letisha?

This could end up in a lawsuit. Would the tape hold up in court as evidence?

The recording was real—and really Gabe—but it hadn't been recorded in Harper's house nor had they captured it on the date Letisha had been there. Could an expert prove that?

As Natalie panicked, Harper continued to lay out her plan of attack against Madame Letisha, unconcerned that neither Stone nor Natalie was participating in the conversation.

"I'll give her a one star on Yelp, of course. But I think I need to go live on social media and play that tape. I'll cross-post the video to every platform I'm on."

The path to Madame Letisha's destruction continued as Harper started to brainstorm how to add the character of a charlatan—a fraud medium—into the current book she was writing. And then how to kill off the character in the most horrible way possible.

"Well that turned dark quickly," Gabe said as Millie watched Harper rant.

He turned his gaze back to Natalie.

"What are you going to do now?" he asked. "Any more brilliant ideas?"

She didn't need snarky sarcastic comments from the resident spirit. But she did need a good idea of what to do to deal with this situation and Harper.

Unfortunately, it seemed she was fresh out of ideas.

Chapter Three

As the ghost world and the world of the living—the two realms Natalie had attempted to navigate separately for the past year—collided, the last thing Natalie needed was to host book club at the shop.

But there was no way to get out of it. Her one and only employee, Jules, was taking a night class and couldn't cover the evening so it fell to Natalie.

If it was a nice normal book club who sat in a circle and talked about the latest read, she could just hide in the shop and wait for them to leave. But there was nothing normal about Mudville, or its residents. Which is why it was no surprise when Alice Mudd, octogenarian and direct descendent of the town's founding family, popped her head in the front door and said, "I need help."

Resigned, Natalie drew in a breath and braced herself for anything. "Coming."

Outside, she saw why Alice, five feet tall maybe on a good day, needed help. She was trying to wrestle her giant beverage dispenser out of the back seat.

Natalie eyed the dispenser suspiciously. "Alice, I thought we agreed you weren't going to serve magic mushroom lemonade at book club anymore."

"I'm not."

Phew. "Good. Thank you," Natalie said as she took the two gallon-sized containers of tea from Alice's hands.

"This is cannabis iced tea," Alice said as she pushed the car door closed with one foot while balancing the empty dispenser on her hip.

"What?" Natalie choked.

"Don't look so scandalized. It's legal here now and I have a bumper crop of weed growing behind the barn to share with my friends."

The question was, knowing Alice, how many friends had she *shared* her weed with but had forgotten to tell them they were being drugged.

Frowning, Natalie remembered the brownies Alice had brought to the last meeting. She'd had only half of one but remembered feeling completely relaxed and mellow. And she'd slept like a baby that night.

Dammit. She'd been drugged by Alice. Again!

"Alice—"

"Agnes needs this tonight. And that's your fault," Alice said, waiting by the door for Natalie to open it for her.

"Why my fault?" she asked, while juggling the two gallons of pot tea and opening the door.

"You told her the house is haunted. Poor Agnes hasn't slept in two days."

Crap. The lie that had been meant to keep this whole ghost thing under wraps had done the opposite. Blown up and spread all over town.

She should have known. This was Mudville. Small town at its best—and worst. Gossip spread like wildfire and so did lies—and truths.

The last thing she'd wanted to do was freak out Harper's great aunt Agnes over the ghost living in her house. The worst part was, Millie had actually moved out. The house was now ghost free for the first time in a hundred years. Agnes really did have nothing to worry about—not that she'd believe that.

Maybe it was a good thing Alice came prepared to dose the book club. At least Agnes might sleep tonight.

The regular book club crowd filtered in and every

one of them stopped at the refreshment table for a cup of Alice's iced tea.

One day they were going to get in trouble for this. As she smiled and greeted each attendee, Natalie imagined DEA and SWAT descending upon the old train depot turned book and wine shop and cuffing her. Cuffing them all—Alice included.

She'd have a record. And a mug shot!

Liam would have to bail her out. He'd never let her hear the end of it.

As she imagined the worst, the meeting had begun in the next room. Steering clear of the beverage area, Natalie hovered near the back to make sure the club didn't need anything from her before she went back to the shop to try and get some cardboard boxes broken down for recycling.

"Before we get started on the book discussion, I wanted to run an idea past everyone," Alice began, apparently running tonight's meeting instead of Agnes, who truly didn't look well. Guilt weighed on Natalie's shoulders.

Meanwhile Alice shushed two attendees who weren't completely silent.

She was in rare form today, standing in front of the group, but barely tall enough for Natalie to see her over the heads of those seated in the room.

"The recent situation that Agnes has found herself in," there was a murmur in the room that Alice quickly silenced with one sharp glance, "has given me an idea."

Natalie noticed that Alice hadn't elaborated as to what Agnes's situation was exactly but everyone seemed to know anyway. Small town. Zero secrets.

"We're going to use this as an opportunity to put Mudville on the map."

What?

"You know we've all been writing to Hallmark to get them to film one of those Christmas movies here, to no avail. But Hallmark's loss is the Paranormal Channel's gain. Now I don't approve of how it seems they've gone all in on crappy reality television, but I can forgive that if they choose Mudville as the location for their new show."

The low murmur of chatter began again as Natalie wondered what the hell Alice was talking about.

"They're holding a contest. The winner gets to be the location for their new show. Harper, if you would be so kind." Alice glanced up and found where Harper was seated.

Harper stood, a stack of cards in one hand and a fist of pens in the other. "As Alice said, PNC is accepting nominations for the town for their next location. So all we have to do is fill out these postcards.

I've already printed all the information for the town and stamped and addressed them to the channel. All you have to do is sign your name and add your information in the return address field."

"Do you think we really have a chance to be chosen?" Mary Brimley asked.

"Of course, we do. They'd be foolish not to choose us," Margaret Trout sniped.

"Hallmark hasn't," Dee Flanders reminded them. "And we've been emailing them for a year."

"Right. Because they're foolish." Margaret nodded.

Agnes had stayed conspicuously quiet until now. Alice moved to stand behind her chair. The diminutive woman squeezed her friend's shoulder and said, "I think we have an excellent chance of being chosen. Right, Agnes?"

Agnes let out a breath but bobbed her head in agreement as Natalie wondered what any of this Paranormal Channel stuff had to do with poor Agnes.

"What's the show they'd be filming?" Mary, the town's ad hoc information officer and chief keeper of all Mudville knowledge, asked.

"That's the reason we're a shoo-in. Between Agnes's house and Harper's evidence they'll have no choice but to choose Mudville, because the name of the show is..." Flashing yellowing teeth in what took on the vestiges of an evil grin, Alice revealed after a lengthy dramatic pause, "*Ghost House*."

Ghost House. At that the air left Natalie's lungs.

Her nightmare was coming true.

She'd lied to prevent exactly this. Prevent strangers and looky-loos from invading Mudville on their amateur ghost hunts. And now it was going to happen anyway.

Chapter Four

THE MONTHS PASSED QUICKLY, AS TIME seemed to do the older Natalie got.

Before she knew it, the searing heat of summer had slipped away. There was a crispness to the air most mornings, which got chased away by noon as the autumn sun warmed the old brick depot that was her home and work.

The trees along Main Street changed, their summer leaves of verdant green turning to burnished shades of red, yellow and bronze.

The arrival of autumn was her favorite time of year since she'd moved upstate.

This year, especially. The application deadline for the dreaded *Ghost House* show had passed in September—she knew because she'd stalked the PNC website closely—and there'd been no word from the network.

Hopefully that meant that Alice and Harper's postcard writing campaign to get Mudville chosen as the Paranormal Channel *Ghost House* host town had failed.

That was not a surprise. The romance and the mystery book clubs were strong and active, but their ranks still only amounted to barely a dozen people. Which was great for a town with only a thousand residents—men, women and children included. But not enough to win a contest, thank goodness.

With that worry beginning to dissipate, the rhythm of Natalie's days remained even. Normal.

Well, normal except for one thing... Gabe.

Natalie glanced out the front window now, looking left and then right to see if Gabe was making his way to the shop.

She hated to admit how disturbed she was that he wasn't there as she opened the store and got ready for the day.

Gabe had always been a creature of habit, as was she. Nearly every day since she'd first begun to be able to see ghosts, he'd been there. Sliding through the front door, hovering by the cash register before she'd even finished her first cup of coffee.

That was *until* that fateful day. The morning after she'd failed to tell Harper the truth.

Gabe had been late arriving that next morning, in spite of knowing she really needed him there, with Millie, so she and Liam could make the fake recording of a real ghost to expose that fraud of a medium, Madame Letisha.

He'd come, but late and not happily. He'd been different since then. Subtle changes but Natalie had noticed. He was still friendly. Still polite. But he wouldn't wander in until the afternoon. Or he'd skip visiting her in the store altogether.

She'd assumed he was just busy with his relationship. His and Millie's was a love story for the ages. Both souls trapped in this earthly purgatory rather than moving on. Both murdered, though one hundred years apart.

But Natalie managed to maintain a relationship with Liam and not completely abandon her friends. As a ghost with no responsibilities—no job, no bills to pay, no laundry to do, no toilets to scrub—certainly Gabe could juggle friends and a love life too.

A part of her suspected Gabe was annoyed with her. Upset because she didn't bare her soul to Harper and Stone that spring day.

It was a long time to hold a grudge.

Easy for him to judge her. No one would stare at *him* the way they definitely were going to stare and point and whisper about her if she told the truth.

She could imagine quite well how it would go. It had haunted her ever since she'd even considered telling Harper.

There goes that crazy woman who thinks she can talk to ghosts.

Or *there's that shop owner who lied about seeing the dead just to get attention and more business.*

Her life in Mudville would be forever altered... as if it hadn't been already by her unwilling acquisition of this ability. Power. *Curse...*

A sound outside had Natalie whipping her gaze toward the street, or what she could see of it through the shop's front windows.

What the hell was that? Hooves?

A horse. And it was traveling *fast*—or at least that's what it sounded like to her transplanted city girl ears.

She had seen a horse and buggy last year after moving to Mudville. That day she'd whipped out her cell phone and recorded the sighting. She'd immediately texted Harper, Red and Bethany who, like indulgent mothers in the face of an unnecessarily excited child, explained she'd likely have more Amish sightings as they sometimes traveled from the next county to Mudville for the weekly stock sales.

But that horse, though traveling along at an impressive clip in front of its driver and buggy, hadn't sounded as if it was barreling down Main Street like it was the final stretch of the Kentucky Derby. This horse sounded like it was hauling ass.

She shoved open the front door and rushed out onto the sidewalk. By the time she ran to the side street to get a view of Main Street, the sound was gone.

Maybe she shouldn't think anything of the occurrence. There was a good chance it wasn't even an anomaly.

Mudville was in some ways very old fashioned, while in other ways being right on the cutting edge of modern times. An odd duality encapsulated in one tiny village.

There were farmers who sold their crops along the side of the road to tourists and locals alike. While not too far down that road was a building running three shifts manufacturing, for instance, components for the International Space Station.

But Mudville wasn't *ride your horse to the store* kind of small or old fashioned.

There was a good chance it had just been some farm kids messing around. Racing their horse down

Main Street on a dare. Or maybe it was a horse that had gotten loose from a nearby farm. In that case she hoped someone caught it before it got hurt.

With a new worry added to her list—the possible runaway horse's welfare—she turned back toward the shop...and came face-to-face with Gabe. Arms crossed. Face stern.

As happy as she was to see him after the recent dearth in visitations, she knew that was his lecture face.

He had something to say. Or more accurately something to complain about.

Fine. But they were going to do this inside next to her coffee.

"Good morning, Gabe. Come on in." She said it in a tone as bright and sunny as the smile she flashed him and reached for the doorknob.

Gabe, of course, just walked through the window and met her inside, where he once again blocked her way.

Nope. Not gonna happen. Coffee first. Ghost complaints second.

She walked straight at him.

When he didn't move and there wasn't room between the front table of books and the shelves next to it for her to pass, she continued—straight through him.

"Whoa. Since when do you walk *through* me?" he griped, sounding honestly shocked.

"Since you're blocking my way before I've drank my coffee."

He rolled his eyes. Judgmental, this morning, wasn't he?

Finally in possession of her insulated mug—an attempt to keep her beverage at least some semblance of hot since she got interrupted so much—she took a long sip.

She closed her eyes and enjoyed the first bracing swallow.

Opening her eyes again, she turned her focus to Gabe, whose impatient side was showing.

She'd think a guy who had eternity would be less uptight. Show more patience.

Brows raised, she said, "Proceed. What's your grievance today?"

He scowled. "What's that supposed to mean?"

"Nothing, Cranky McCrankster. Talk. What did you want?" she asked, wondering if he really didn't know he'd been acting differently toward her lately. Or if it was all part of his plan to drive her to confess to Harper.

Or maybe he'd had a fight with his ghost girlfriend,

since Millie wasn't with him now. Who knew? It wasn't like he told her anything anymore.

Legs planted wide, he crossed his arms over his chest again. Dressed as he was, in the explorer-slash-adventurer outfit in which he'd died, Gabe looked every bit like a poster for an Indiana Jones movie, sans whip.

"It's October first—"

"Oh, crap," she interrupted.

The month had changed when she wasn't looking, yet again. It was past time she'd decorated the shop for fall. Not to mention spooky season. The ghosts of Mudville took Halloween very seriously. She'd learned that last year.

"I'm sorry, Gabe. Tell everyone I'll get the shop decorated for Halloween today. I promise."

He shook his head. "It's not that. I mean yes, please do. You're late already in my opinion. Red's had Halloween stuff out in her shop since the first week of August. But that's not what this is about."

"You shop at Red's?" she asked, feeling a little hurt and jealous.

"No, Natalie, I do not *shop* at Red's," Gabe began, as if she were a five-year-old who needed something explained to her. "I'm a ghost. I have no money nor can I change my clothes."

She let out a sigh. "You know what I mean. I didn't know you hung out there."

"A lot of us do...since you won't allow any of them inside *your* shop..."

Insult noted, point taken, and summarily ignored.

She continued, "So what are you upset about if not my lack of holiday spirit?"

"You promised you'd tell Harper and Stone."

Yup. She'd been right. Gabe's bad mood was about this.

"It's been *months* since then and you still haven't done it."

"It hasn't been all that long," she began.

"You promised in late May. I remember because you were bitching that Stone wouldn't plant the annuals in your garden that weren't frost-hardy until the last week of May."

She frowned. "I wasn't bitching."

Gabe ignored the comment except to raise one brow above the gaze he leveled on her. He held up one hand and counted on his fingers. "May, June, July, August, September, *October*."

Now it was her turn to roll her eyes. "You can't count October. Today is only the first. And you really can't count May. It was the end of the month."

She remembered too and Gabe was right. Stone had been working on finally finishing her new Victorian garden in the side yard that day when he'd heard Gabe and Millie speaking and freaked out.

"So your argument is that it's only been *four* months since you made a promise you didn't keep and not six?" His brow quirked higher, disappearing beneath the brim of his hat.

"It's easy for you to talk. You're not the one everyone is going to think is crazy or a liar because you see the dead."

"Yeah, because it's so easy for me actually *being* one of the dead."

She swore that if he rolled his eyes one more time at her she was going to toss the nearest book at him. Not that it would do anything but fly through him. But he'd get the idea she was getting angry at least.

"Why are you so upset about this? Why is it so important to you anyway?" she asked.

Harper wasn't Gabe's friend. He wasn't the one having to lie and hide things from her.

"Millie misses living in Agnes's house. She wants to move back in but it's too risky since everyone can hear us when we're together."

Natalie cringed as she inadvertently pictured Gabe

and Millie being *together*—as in the Biblical sense of the word—and what Harper might possibly hear.

She pushed that image far, far away and said, "Why does she want to move back in? She was *murdered* in that house."

"That house has also been her only home for the past hundred years," Gabe said.

Natalie drew in a breath and let it out. "All right. I get it. But isn't there someplace else—somewhere new —you two can go? Someplace that isn't just hers but both of yours," she suggested, thinking it sounded reasonable. Romantic even. "What about the mansion on the hill? I thought you liked it there."

He shook his head. "Too crowded. Everybody's always hanging out there. It's like a frat house up there now."

"Oh." She cringed again in commiseration with the unfortunate owners of the beautiful property, who'd unwittingly had their home become ghost party central.

"Look, Nat. I do everything you ask of me—"

"Do you?" She scoffed.

His face hardened. "I made that fake recording you tricked Harper with."

The recording which had saved Natalie from

having to confess but had also sent Harper down a ghost-filled rabbit hole, Alice Mudd and the mystery book club members going with her.

In hindsight, Natalie should have considered other options...

She sighed. "I know."

"Why can't you even consider doing this for me?" he asked, his tone as hard as his countenance.

How quickly he'd forgotten all she'd already done for him. Like the fact she'd solved his murder, at great personal risk to herself and Liam. Not to mention ensuring his relatives inherited Gabe's lifelong collection of treasures.

Since he seemed to be keeping score, that all should count in her favor.

"Please," he added, softening.

She met his gaze. "Gabe, you know how I feel about you. You're my best friend."

Liam didn't count. He was her boyfriend. It was different.

"And you're mine," Gabe echoed, warming her heart as she feared he might not feel the same. Or at least not anymore.

"But Gabe. I'm sorry, but I can't do this. I can't do what you're asking."

He paused for a second then nodded. "All right, Nat. You do what you gotta do."

When he turned and left through the front wall she wondered if she might have just lost her best friend.

Chapter Five

"YOU ALL RIGHT?" LIAM ASKED, HIS ARM around her shoulders as they watched television.

"I'm fine." Which was true except that she'd been having to endure his picking apart the show she'd chosen for them to watch.

"You're quiet," he said, watching her now instead of the screen.

She let out a wry laugh. "You should be grateful for that."

He narrowed his eyes as if evaluating her. "What happened today? Something in the shop?"

Of all the times she'd wished Liam would be more present and observant, now was not one of them. "Nothing happened."

"Natalie..."

"What are you a mind reader now?"

"Apparently I am a ghost hunter now, at least according to Harper who is so impressed by my tape recording. Mind reader is the next logical step, I figure. Do you think Madame Letisha has an opening for an apprentice?" A cocky, crooked smile quirked up one corner of his lips.

She narrowed her eyes at him over the mention of Madame Letisha, in spite of that damn sexy dimple of his showing and making her want to bite his chin.

"Fine. Yes, something happened. Gabe is mad at me for not telling Harper the truth. And I don't know... it's upsetting." She lifted one shoulder.

"Do you get this upset when you and I argue?" Liam asked.

"Do you think you're ever going to stop being jealous of my friendship with Gabe?" she countered.

He screwed up his mouth. "I'm not jealous."

"You sound jealous."

"Well, I'm not." He scowled.

Great. Now they were both upset over Gabe, just for different reasons.

Although she had to admit, Liam had been pretty great. After his initial grumpiness over her not telling Harper and implicating him in her lie and the fake tape, he'd gotten over it.

More importantly, Liam had stood behind her decision to keep her ghost communications quiet. Maybe he was worried he'd be marked as the boyfriend of the loon in town who thought she could talk to dead people. Not that Liam—a loner at heart—had ever been the type to care much about what people said or thought about him. Which was a good thing since half the town had thought he was a serial killer when he'd first moved here with his cadaver lab and the body bags started to show up.

She ran a finger over Liam's muscle. "Hey."

His gaze dropped to her hand on his chest and he said, "Hey."

"Do you wanna... you know?"

His brows shot high. "You're not too upset over Gabe to... *you know*?"

She screwed up her mouth at his being a smart ass. "We don't have to if you don't want to—"

"I want to." Before she could say a word he was on his feet, pulling her to hers.

What had to be hours later, Natalie came awake.

She had the distinct feeling that something had disturbed her. That this was not a normal waking up, even though that so often happened to her in the middle of the night in spite of how tired she was.

As her body came slowly out of sleep, her mind pondered the situation. She wasn't sure what had disturbed her but one thing was for certain. She wasn't happy about it.

It had taken forever for her to finally get to sleep tonight. First because Liam was very thorough in all things he did—sex included. Then, long after he'd fallen to sleep, her mind kept replaying her talk with Gabe that morning.

True to form, her brain always liked to obsess over the worst part of her day just when she needed to sleep.

Worse, falling asleep wasn't her only problem. Getting *back to sleep* without staring at the clock for hours after being awakened in the middle of the night was. That was nearly impossible. It took hours. Because of that Liam had long ago been warned about her feelings on this subject. He knew well not to wake her up for middle of the night sex.

At forty she was old enough to know that sleep was sexy. Not being exhausted all day. Sexy. Not having shadows under her eyes. Sexy.

But her awakening tonight had nothing to do with Liam. He slept like the dead next to her. Not moving. Breathing so softly she could barely hear him. As usual.

His being a good sleeper—and not a snorer—was the only reason she allowed him to stay overnight at her place. Okay, maybe his sleeping like the dead wasn't the *only* reason she let him stay in her bed.

The multiple orgasms from earlier tonight were a big reason why he slept over most nights—when he wasn't working all hours of the night on his research project at the lab. And in the cold weather, he was like having a furnace in bed with her to snuggle up to. Which was why in the summer, or right now while they were still having mild early fall weather, she had the ceiling fan in the bedroom turned on.

That fan currently produced a nice, cool, soothing breeze as it brushed against her face. That was another good thing about Liam—besides his hot body. He was good at doing stuff. Stuff like hanging fans in hundred and twenty year old buildings with tin ceilings.

Ting.

She frowned as the odd sound interrupted her thought. It sent her mind spinning as she tried to place what the noise was.

It couldn't have been Mr. Darcy. The uninvited squatter of a cat who'd claimed the renovated train-station as his home slept in the front of the building, on top of the shelves in the book shop. Not back here in the part she'd fixed up as an apartment.

Ting.

There it was again.

It was almost like a soft metal sound. Not loud like a bell, but small like the gentlest clink of a spoon against a champagne glass—which was ridiculous. Who would be clinking glasses around here now?

Gabe and all the ghosts knew none of them were allowed in her apartment under penalty of death—so to speak. This was her sacred space.

Besides, in all the time she'd known them, they never went around clinking or clanking anything. Her ghosts were nothing like Scrooge's chain-rattling specters. Thank God.

So what was it then? What was making that noise?

She tried to reason it out.

The sound was coming from above her, near the ceiling. Was it a big fly hitting the tin ceiling over and over again?

Ugh. She stifled a groan. There was nothing worse than wondering. She had to know.

Sleep and Liam be damned. There was a mystery to solve. There was no way around it. She was going to have to turn on the light to figure this thing out.

As she reached out her arm toward the lamp on the side table a series of things occurred, though it was such a confused jumble she couldn't be sure in what order.

There was a kind of a *whack* followed by a *thud* as something—something that felt much larger than a fly —hit the bed.

At the same time she managed to turn on the light, which led to her seeing what had landed on the bed.

That's when the screaming started. Hers, because there was a freaking bat on her bed. And Liam's as he startled awake and yelled, "What's wrong?"

"Bat!" she screamed, somehow managing to form the word.

He cussed but being a military man, he jumped into action.

Liam dispatched with the threat in what felt to her almost in slow motion. He flipped the top edge of the comforter over the still motionless bat. Then proceeded to flip the other three sides of the comforter, forming a kind of bat burrito.

"Oh my God, get it out of here!" she screeched.

"Relax. I got it." His nonchalance didn't make her feel much better.

She was definitely going to have to throw out the comforter. Possibly the ceiling fan too.

She watched as Liam opened the back door and

tossed the whole bundle outside into the night. Then, he went outside and started to unwrap it.

"What are you doing?" She scrambled out of bed to rush to the door. "He could wake up any second and try to fly back in here."

"Then close the door," he said, glancing up as he flipped the final corner of the comforter over to reveal the dark creature—still not moving in the center of the fluffy white bed covering.

Keeping the door mostly closed, she peered through a two-inch crack and asked, "Is it dead?"

"It's probably just stunned. It must have gotten hit with the blades from the ceiling fan," he explained much too calmly in her opinion.

"Well, get back inside anyway. Before it bites you."

"It's more likely to fly away. They're more afraid of you than—"

"Yeah, yeah. I've heard that all before. I don't care. Get inside."

Liam, barefoot and shirtless in nothing but boxer shorts—he didn't sleep naked mostly because he didn't trust there were no ghosts around to see him—looked damn good in the moonlight. His muscles all hard and bulging.

She started to think about what else could be hard and bulging and suddenly she wanted him inside for a different reason. A completely non-bat related reason.

Opening the door wider, she stepped aside so he could come in. Then, she decided to take one more look at the bat.

Shit. It was gone! She squeaked and slammed the door shut. And then locked it.

Liam glanced back at her. "What's the matter?"

"It's gone."

"Told you it wasn't dead," he said, grabbing the two throws she kept folded on the sofa before heading back to bed. "You'll have to wash that bedding in the morning.

"Or throw it out," she said, while hunching and scanning the ceiling for more aerial predators.

She reached for the pull chain on the fan. She'd rather be hot than whacked with unconscious bats in the night.

Once the fan, which she would forever more think of as a "bat whacker" began to slow to a stop, she walked to Liam as he flipped one throw out, letting it float down onto the sheet below.

She pressed against his back as she wrapped her arms around him. She needed comfort and a distraction after this horrifying scare. "So as long as we're awake anyway…"

He turned in her arms, dark brows cocked high.

"There's a rule. *Your* rule. No middle of the night sex. Remember?" He smirked, even as she felt something besides his muscles bulging against her.

"Technically, the rule is no *waking me up* for middle of the night sex. You didn't. The bat did. So..."

He reached down, palmed her bottom and lifted her up. She squeaked again, wrapping her legs around his waist.

"So technically, I guess this is okay," he said.

"Definitely okay," she agreed as he tossed her onto the mattress.

Chapter Six

It was the morning of the monthly ghost council meeting—which was one more thing Natalie did for Gabe that he seemed to have forgotten yesterday.

Last year when he'd told her the ghosts wanted to meet with her regularly to have their say she had agreed. Even with as weird as it was and even if it did mean getting up an hour early to host the meeting before the shop opened for the day.

She hadn't seen him since their falling out—if she could call it that—the day before. He'd be there for the meeting though. Ricky, who'd declared himself chairperson of the ghost coalition, wouldn't look kindly on Gabe's absence.

As she poured the coffee into her mug, she was

anxious to see what Gabe's attitude would be this morning.

"Hey." Liam's sleep gruff voice near her ear as he wrapped his arms around her from behind sent a thrill down her spine.

"Good morning. You slept late, for you." Natalie was used to Liam being up before her.

"Someone kept me up last night," he said, nuzzling her throat.

"Speaking of the bat, can you toss the comforter in the garbage bin when you leave?"

"I wasn't speaking of the bat, but yes, I will toss the comforter," he said.

His hand creeping lower to palm her stomach reminded her of what had them both up late the night before—besides the bat.

"You're up early too," he said.

"Ghost council."

"Ah, yes. How could I forget? I'm going to bow out of this one if that's okay with you." He reached around her and snagged her coffee cup, taking a big sip.

"That's fine," she said, stealing the mug back with a frown. "I don't think Ricky will be upset."

"Good. Wouldn't want Ricky to get upset." Liam rolled his eyes.

He'd never actually seen Rick and he could only

hear Gabe and Millie, so she could imagine ghost meetings were pretty boring for Liam. That hadn't stopped her from demanding he be there for them for the first few months though.

Liam reached for a ceramic mug from the shelf to pour his own cup since she obviously wasn't willing to share hers. Smart man.

She had to go anyway, if only to avoid a nasty look from Ricky for being late. "I'd better—*Agh!*"

The bat came out of nowhere, heading directly at her head.

She dropped to the floor while managing to save the cup in her hand.

Liam frowned down at her. "What are you doing?"

"Bat!"

"Natalie. There is no bat."

Oh yes, there was. What the hell was Liam talking about? "It almost hit me in the head!"

"Nat. I'm standing right here. I would have seen it."

"You weren't looking."

"I'm looking now. Where is it?" he asked.

She glanced around from her squatting position on the floor. Admittedly she didn't see it right then, but that didn't mean she hadn't seen it before. She most certainly had. And she supposed she shouldn't be surprised. Where there was one, there was bound to be more—as horrifying as that concept was.

Reaching up she grabbed the edge of the counter with one hand and pulled herself up, still hunching low just in case. All the while Liam sipped his coffee with an amused expression.

"It was here," she said, standing slightly straighter.

"I'm sure it was. Better get to your meeting. I'm heading to the lab."

"Fine," she grumbled, accepting his quick kiss but not his condescending tone.

There *was* a bat. He'd see she was right, eventually, even if she really didn't want to be.

Chapter Seven

ANNOYED ALREADY AND IT WAS BARELY NINE in the morning, Natalie made her way to the room she'd allotted in the shop to be used for book club meetings.

The ghosts were already there, filling the seats comprised of the used furniture she'd gotten from Red's Resale shop.

Gabe sat on the sofa. Ricky in the wooden chair at the head of what was usually a refreshment table. Harriet, who'd been lucky enough to die of natural causes at a ripe old age, perched in the upholstered chair, which left the matching seat open for Natalie.

Ricky eyed her before pointedly glancing at the grandfather clock in the corner.

She followed his gaze and frowned. "That clock runs fast."

It showed her five minutes late when the time on her cell said she was right on time.

"Mm-hm." Ricky scowled.

"It does!" With a scowl of her own, she leaned back in her chair.

No use arguing smartphone accuracy versus that of antique time pieces with a man who'd taken two shots to the chest for allegedly cheating at cards well over a decade before the first iPhone had been released. But she could argue this...

"Where's Train Track Tim?" she asked. "He's late too."

"Tim's visiting friends in Afton," Ricky informed her.

Although how Tim, who lacked a jaw—train accident—had conveyed that information to him, she couldn't guess.

After pointedly drawing his gaze away from Natalie, Ricky addressed the others in the room. "Now that we're finally all here, I officially call our monthly meeting of the Mudville Ghost Council to order at nine-oh-six a.m.."

It wasn't really nine-oh-six, but whatever. She

leaned back in the chair, crossed her arms and held tight to her coffee cup.

"Do we have any new business?" Ricky asked, glancing around the room.

First of all, how had this meeting gotten so official? She should have nipped the formalities in the bud months ago, rather than letting Ricky and the ghosts have their way. Too late now.

But as a matter of fact, she did have some new business.

"I do." Natalie raised her hand, somehow succumbing to the official feel of this meeting.

"The chair recognizes Natalie."

"Thank you. There was this horse galloping down Main Street—"

Ricky nodded. "I saw."

Of course he would. His home base, so to speak, was in the old cemetery on Main Street.

"Okay. So do we know who the horse belongs to? It could have gotten loose from one of the farms. In which case I hope the owner secured how it got out before it gets hurt on Main Street—"

Ricky snorted. "It's not going to get hurt."

Relieved, she asked, "So it had a rider?"

"Oh, yes." He nodded.

Ricky wasn't being all that forthcoming, so she asked, "Who owns it?"

"There's no owner, Nat," Gabe said.

"It's a ghost horse," Harriet finally explained when the men weren't more helpful.

Natalie's eyes widened. "A *ghost* horse?"

Holy shit! As if seeing human ghosts wasn't enough, now there were animal ghosts as well?

And if there were, why was this the first she was seeing one? These were the kind of questions she would have normally asked Gabe, except he was being less communicative than usual.

"Those exist?" she asked, grateful she had the rest of the ghost council to ask. They were still talking to her at least.

Ricky nodded. "Yes, they exist."

She swallowed, a little afraid to ask this question, but she did anyway. "And the rider?"

"I didn't see it, but it's probably Sybil," Harriet said, with a glance at the others in the room, who nodded.

"Sybil is the horse?" Natalie asked, at a loss.

"No, Sybil Ludington, the human, riding her horse. She's been known to be seen riding around here close to Halloween," Ricky explained.

"So she's a ghost too?" Natalie asked, just trying to get her facts straight.

After a huff, Gabe said, "Natalie, what do you think would happen if you sat on a ghost horse?"

"I'd pass right through."

"Exactly." He threw his hands in the air.

"She is a ghost too, yes," Harriet said, much more diplomatically.

All right, so maybe it had been a silly question. That didn't mean Gabe had to get so snippy about it.

"I'm sorry but I've never heard of this Sybil. And I thought it was the headless horseman who rode on Halloween," she said, glancing around the room.

"The headless horseman is a Hessian soldier from the Revolutionary War and only rides in Sleepy Hollow," Gabe said.

"And that is only a legend, as far as I know. This is Sybil Ludington. And she's very real," Harriet added.

When Natalie showed no recognition of the name, Gabe continued, "She's the sixteen-year-old girl version of Paul Revere. In 1777 she rode forty miles from her home in New York to rally her father's troops against the British. She died right here in this very town in 1839."

She shook her head. "You can spew all the dates at

me you want but I'm telling you I've never heard of her."

Gabe, a former history teacher—before his death—scowled. "Pick up a book once in a while, Nat. You're surrounded by more books than half of the spirits in the graveyard had ever seen during the entire duration of their lifetimes and all you read—when you read at all—are trashy romance novels."

She narrowed her eyes at him.

Pick on her for not reading more. Fine. She was overworked and tired but yes, she could pick up a book rather than reach for the television remote control at the end of a long day. Agreed. Guilty. But do *not* slam the romance genre.

She was about to lecture him about that when it hit her. The possible reason for Gabe's foul mood.

"Where's Millie?" she asked.

He drew back at the abrupt change of subject. "What?"

"I haven't seen you with Millie lately. And she's not here now. Where is she? Oh my God. You two didn't break up, did you? Is that why you're so cranky?"

"No. We didn't break up. And I'm not cranky." Gabe scowled.

The rest of the spirits reacted to various degrees

that indicated they agreed more with Natalie's assessment than with Gabe's denial.

"She's just visiting her family in Sharon Springs," he explained defensively.

"Wait. She can travel? I thought you all couldn't move from where your body was."

Natalie remembered the two female ghosts tethered to their bodies in Liam's lab. They'd left—thank God—when he'd sent their cadavers back to wherever bodies donated to science went. And not a moment too soon. It seemed their only pastimes had been being rude to Natalie and spying on Liam.

"It seems like the closer we get to Halloween, the more leeway we have," Ricky explained. "Which is why Sybil, who's buried a couple of hours drive from here, can travel back here to where she died. But only during October."

"Yes," Harriet agreed. "It feels like the period of time that starts right around the first day of autumn straight through to All Saints Day—"

"Or *Día de Muertos*," Ricky added.

Harriet nodded and continued, "—extends our boundaries, so to speak."

The rules of the ghost world were still very hazy to her, and to them apparently too, based on how they were talking. She was still going to try to talk to Gabe alone. Make sure he was just missing his girlfriend and it was nothing more serious… and now she was a ghost relationship counselor too. Too bad she wasn't getting paid for any of this.

"Next on the agenda—" Ricky began.

"Wait? We have an agenda now?" Natalie asked, guessing that her business had officially been dismissed.

A fast rapping on the window interrupted whatever Ricky had on his ghost agenda. Natalie whipped her head around to see Alice Mudd, pressed against the glass peering in like a kid at a candy store.

Ricky let out a huff at the interruption.

"I have to deal with Alice," she said out of the side of her mouth, hoping Alice couldn't see her speaking, again, to no one.

"Go ahead." Rick scowled.

What did he have to be upset about? She was the one who looked like she was sitting in the meeting room alone talking aloud to herself. Maybe she should just tell people the truth. At times like this it almost seemed easier than all the lying.

Chapter Eight

Ignoring Rick's cranky mood, which wasn't much better than Gabe's, Natalie stood.

She had more important things to worry about than Rick. Such as what would have Alice knocking on her door almost an hour before the shop opened?

"Good morning, Alice," she greeted with as much enthusiasm as she could muster. "It's not ten yet."

"Get out of the way, girl. I'm not here to shop. We have important things to discuss." Alice pushed past her and into the meeting room. "And why are you sitting in here by yourself anyway?"

"I was, um, doing my... morning meditation."

"Well, meditate on this. They chose the venue for *Ghost House*." As she announced it, Alice moved to flop back into the chair currently occupied by Harriet.

"No!" Leaping forward, Natalie grabbed both of Alice's arms and pivoted the diminutive woman toward the empty chair she'd vacated. "Sit here. That other chair has a horrible spring problem."

Once Alice was seated, Natalie perched on the edge of the coffee table and let out a breath. "Now what were you saying about *Ghost House*?" she asked.

"They didn't choose Mudville," Alice announced with a scowl.

"Oh, no. That's terrible. I'm so upset." Natalie ignored Gabe's snort over her poor acting.

"I am upset. It would have been fun," Rick commented.

Harriet shook her head. "I don't know. All those strangers in town."

Unaware of the conversation happening around her, Alice continued, "They chose a supposedly haunted theater in Utica. *Humph*. What a racket. They didn't even have a ghost voice on tape the way we did."

"I am sorry, Alice. I know you're disappointed after how hard you worked to get Mudville on the show." That, at least, was the truth.

Alice waved one hand. "That's the least of my concerns. You won't believe who they hired to lead the cast."

Natalie shook her head. "I couldn't even guess."

"That fake Madame Letisha!"

Harper's discredit campaign had spread the word far and wide—or at least to the Mudville town line—about how Madame Letisha was a fraud. Alice was visibly upset over the choice and Natalie couldn't blame her.

Was there no justice? Letisha was no better than a grifter. An overt scammer.

She lied for a living and the Paranormal Channel was going to put her on television and make her a household name for doing it? Okay, Natalie did a good bit of lying herself but she didn't take people's money for it.

Letisha's business would skyrocket. She'd be able to peddle her fake clairvoyant medium services and swindle innocent trusting people all across the country. People who might be depending on her for actual help with a ghost problem.

"What are you going to do about it?" Natalie asked knowing Alice was not the type to sit quietly and let things pass. Not when she was this riled up.

More knocking on the window had Natalie and the ghosts glancing at the front of the shop one more time.

Harper stood there yelling through the glass, "Oh my God! Did you hear? Madame Letisha!"

"So much for our meeting," Rick grumbled.

Gabe let out a short laugh. "The meeting can wait. This is far more entertaining."

Natalie shot Gabe a glare for that comment as she stood to unlock the door again for Harper.

Harper stormed inside, saying as she walked, "We can't let that charlatan get famous off this show."

"I agree," Natalie nodded. "But what can we do? Write more letters?"

"Or... we put our own ghost whisperer up for the cast and have her shame that con artist," Alice said, and she stared directly at Natalie as she said it.

She felt the blood drain from her face. How could they know? Who had told? Did Gabe use his and Millie's new ability to be heard to tattle on her?

As Natalie's brain spun as she feared she might pass out from lack of oxygen, because she might have stopped breathing even though her heart was pounding like a racehorse, Harper grabbed her shoulders.

"Yes! You have to apply. You were so good leading that seance last Halloween," Harper said.

Thinking playing dumb was the best course of action—for lack of a better plan—Natalie asked, "Why me? Harper, you're the one writing the ghost book. A famous author with a social media following. They'll love you."

"Hell, I'll apply too. You too, Alice. And Agnes. We all should. Can you picture Letisha's reaction when she sees us all there knowing we know she's running a scam?"

As Alice agreed with Harper, the ghosts in the room carried on their own conversation.

"Now I do wish they'd chosen Mudville. This is going to be one hell of a show," Harriet said.

"Is Utica too far for us to go watch?" Gabe asked.

"Not sure. I never tried traveling that far. They'd have to be filming close to Halloween for us to have any chance at all of making it," Rick commented.

"Can they get a show cast and in production that quickly?" Harriet asked.

Natalie noticed that all three of the ghosts were now looking to her for an answer. Meanwhile she was having a hard enough time keeping track of both conversations happening simultaneously.

To keep the spirit coalition happy, and probably the livings as well, she drew in a breath and asked, "Do you know when they'll start filming?"

"In a couple of weeks. The cast will be locked in the theater for a week. Four days of filming, then the final episode will be broadcast live on Halloween night," Alice explained.

"Not really a ghost *house* though, is it? Since it's in a *theater*." Harper was obviously still upset that a location within Mudville hadn't been chosen, until she grabbed Natalie's arms excitedly. "Nat, you have to apply with me. *Please*."

The invisible peanut gallery behind Harper all watched and waited for her answer just as Harper and Alice did.

Natalie didn't want to do it. Subject herself to not only the audition process and the possibility of rejection. Or worse, get on the cast and have to be locked in a haunted theater with an unknown number of ghosts and Madame Letisha. For a week! Then have to be on live television, when the last time she'd tried that she'd frozen and made a fool of herself in front of the entire WBNG viewing area.

It all sounded like the seventh circle of hell.

There were so many reasons not to do this and only one real reason to do it. Exposing Madame Letisha as a fraud.

Apparently that one reason was enough.

"Okay, I'll do it."

There was rejoicing all around—from both the

living and the dead. Even Gabe smiled. She'd made everyone happy. But she had to wonder what making everyone else happy was going to cost her in the end.

Chapter Nine

It had to be two weeks later, maybe closer to three. Gabe had been acting almost normal since the council meeting. He was there daily at the shop bright and early every day. Often returning late in the evening to keep her company as she closed up—like he had tonight.

That's the way things had been between them since the ghost council meeting. Or, more likely, since Gabe had witnessed her succumb to the peer pressure levied upon her by Alice Mudd and Harper and agreed to apply to be on that Paranormal Channel show about ghosts.

That meant one of two things in her mind. One, Gabe actually believed she'd get on the cast of *Ghost House* and thought that would force her to confess her ghost powers to everyone like he'd always wanted. Or two, he was really bored and lonely because Millie was still away on her annual October visit to her family in Sharon Springs.

For his sake Natalie hoped it was the latter because if Gabe's renewed attentiveness to their friendship was because of the promise of that PNC show, it was bound to be short lived.

There was no way in hell she was going to get chosen to be in the cast. And even if she were by some miracle cast, her two sole goals for being on that show would be to first, expose Madame Letisha as a fraud ghost medium while second, *not* exposing herself as the real deal.

Either way, Gabe was bound to be disappointed if the show was his only reason for forgiving her for not keeping her promise to confess those many months ago.

All she knew was that with Liam working so many hours at the cadaver lab dissecting brains—just the thought made her shiver—she was happy to have her happy-go-lucky, sometimes annoying friend back in her life. She'd just have to enjoy Gabe coming around for however long it lasted.

"Heard any ghost horses lately?" Gabe asked

cockily as he moved to lean against the wall but straightened again before he did.

Finally, a year after being murdered, he was remembering he was dead and could pass—or fall—right through walls. She'd seen that happen too many times to count.

Although since he was being a smart-ass teasing her about the ghost horse, she wouldn't have minded seeing it happen one more time. It would serve him right.

Exactly why did she like having him around so much again?

She shot him a narrow-eyed glare as she put a stack of new releases she'd just unboxed on the front book table. "No, I haven't. And how come that was the first animal ghost I'd ever seen anyway?"

"How do you know it's the first?" he asked.

"What do you mean?"

"I mean if you see a cat or a dog, how do you know they're not ghosts? You thought I was a living when you first met me."

"Well, I know Taco and Mr. Darcy are alive because everyone else sees them. And that annoying crow who hangs out on the roof and terrorizes all my customers too."

"Yes, but what about all the other animals you see around town?"

"I guess I never thought about it."

Maybe that squirrel who amazingly made it across the road right in front of cars but never got hit was actually roadkill turned ghost. It was a mind-blowing concept. She'd never look at another animal the same again.

"But to your point," Gabe began in what she'd come to recognize as his professor tone. "I do believe animal spirits trapped here in... whatever this is, are rare."

She wondered why that was and was about to question his comment when a dark blur zipped across the ceiling.

"Jeezus!" She dropped to the ground, taking shelter under the book table.

When she found Gabe squatting next to her she said, "You saw that too, right?"

"Yes. It's a freaking bat."

"Why are you hiding? It'll just pass right through you. It can't bite you or get tangled in your hair." Both possibilities were lifelong fears of hers. A nightmare coming to life.

"Just because it can pass through me doesn't mean I want it too. *Ick.*" He gave a little shudder.

"At least you saw it. Liam told me I was imagining things the other morning."

"You are most definitely not imagining that." Gabe moved enough that he could peer out from under their cover, glancing up from beneath the brim of his hat to watch the bat circle the shop.

"What am I going to do? I can't have a bat in my shop. It's a danger to the customers. If any even come inside now. After they see that thing swooping around the ceiling it'll be a ghost town in here—no offense."

"None taken. And I guess you call animal control or— Oh. Um, Nat. I don't think you have to worry about the customers seeing the bat."

"Why not? Did it get out?" She tried to see without sacrificing any bit of her shelter and exposing herself to the creature.

Was there a hole somewhere in the ceiling? Did it fly outside through the same mysterious spot that the cat kept using to get in and out of the shop?

"It just flew right through the front window," Gabe answered, standing up. "It's a frigging ghost bat."

Wide-eyed she remembered the bat in the bedroom weeks ago. Getting whacked by the ceiling fan must have been too much for him. It had to have died of internal injuries and then—of all the rotten luck—it decided to haunt her building.

"A ghost bat," she repeated.

Crap. That was going to be impossible to get rid of. There was no ghost animal control, though now she wished there were. But at least it explained why Liam didn't see it that morning and she did. And, one more plus, the customers wouldn't be able to see it.

"A ghost bat, and that means he *can* hit me in the head and won't pass through me, which would be even more unpleasant." Gabe reached down to help her up, then remembering that wouldn't work with her being alive and him dead, he withdrew his hand. With a huff, he said, "Sorry."

"It's okay. Thanks, anyway," she said as she used the table to help her stand.

She'd gotten to her feet just as Alice Mudd crashed against the front door startling them both. Jeez. How many more scares would she have to endure in one night?

Alice kind of bounced off it, realized it was locked since it was just after six, then began to use her fist to pound on the door.

"Hang on, Alice." So much for getting out of there anytime soon. She knew she should have waited to put those books on the front table until the morning.

Natalie flipped the deadbolt and Alice burst in like a whirlwind saying, "You're on."

"On what?" she asked.

"On the show. You got cast!"

The show? As in *Ghost House*? Natalie frowned. "How do you know?"

Did they post the cast online already?

"They mailed you," Alice said.

Natalie frowned deeper as she, for the first time since Alice's grand entrance, noticed the envelopes clutched in the old woman's hand. "Did you open my mail?"

"No, the post lady just handed it to me right outside." Alice thrust the stack of junk mail and bills at her. "The acceptances came in the other kind of mail."

Other kind of mail? Like by Fed Ex?

Confused, she was about to inquire what other kind of mail Alice meant when Harper skidded to a stop and pushed open the front door.

Harper pinned Alice with her gaze. "Did you already tell her? And how did you get here faster than me?"

"Battery-power, baby. My new electric trike goes twenty miles per hour," Alice bragged.

"You both know I got on the show?" Natalie asked. "How?"

Harper cringed. "I'm so sorry, Nat, but once I saw my acceptance I couldn't stand it. I had to check yours.

So I logged into the shop's email account to see if you got accepted too. And you did! Go check your email."

Ah, *that* other kind of mail.

Natalie guessed this was what she got for giving Harper the log-in to the business email account when she'd watched the shop with Jules so she and Liam could get away together.

She was still trying to digest all the information coming at her in rapid fire over the course of less than five minutes. She was on the show. Harper was on the show.

Natalie turned to Alice. "Alice? What about you?"

They'd all applied together. Then, it had seemed like on a lark. Now, not so much.

"I'm in! I texted Harper as soon as I saw I got on. We're gonna be stars! Ooo, have that hottie boyfriend of yours check his mail too."

Natalie shook her head. "No. Remember, Alice, Liam didn't apply."

Harper's aunt Agnes had refused too, along with Stone.

Turns out it was a good thing they hadn't sent in an audition video or they might have been chosen too. Although Natalie couldn't figure out what the producers were looking for in their cast members because she, Harper and Alice couldn't be more different. Although maybe that was exactly the point. What a rag tag group they made.

Natalie shook her head. "I can't believe the three of us made it."

She saw Gabe's satisfied expression as he watched the interaction and, hoping he'd just fall through the wall so she didn't have to see his smug face, angled herself away from him to focus on Harper and Alice.

"I know! It's amazing," Harper agreed with a lot more excitement than Natalie had shown.

"It had to be the videos I submitted for all of us," Alice said.

Natalie turned to Alice. "I thought we all submitted our own videos. I know I did."

"Yup. I saw and they all stunk. That's why I had to fix it."

"Alice," Natalie began, her tone low with suspicion. "What did you do?"

"Give your computer the boot and I'll show you," Alice said, heading toward the cash register where Natalie's shop computer lived on the counter. "The whole casts' audition videos are on the website."

Natalie followed Alice and booted up—or gave it *the boot* as Alice had said—the computer she'd already shut down.

Just fifteen minutes ago she'd been so excited to

be done with her workday. Now she was filled with dread as the screen came to life and she punched in the URL both she and the browser window remembered from her many visits over the past two weeks or so.

And there she was. Listed among those selected for the cast was her picture next to Harper, Alice and—*crap*—Liam.

"Alice! You submitted for Liam?" Natalie asked in shock.

"We needed Hottie McDoc to round out the video. I'm telling you, the video is why we all got on. You gotta tell a story. See? Watch."

Natalie watched in horror as Alice's arthritis riddled finger hit the mouse and the video attached to Liam's photo began to play.

"How did you get all those pictures of him?" Natalie asked.

Including his service photo from when he'd been in the Army.

"It's the age of the internet, Natalie. Everything is online. Keep up," Alice said, pale blue eyes still trained on the video, set to music and with narration, still playing on the computer screen.

It had to have been created by cobbling together still photos, cell phone video and even what looked like doorbell camera footage but the damn thing looked professionally made.

When it ended, Natalie turned to Alice. "How did you do this?"

"I sweet talked that hot young Morgan boy," Alice said proudly.

"Stone's brother Boone?" Harper asked.

Alice nodded. "Yeah, he got his wife to make it."

"Sarah runs a marketing firm," Harper explained to Natalie.

"Anyway, she's a whiz with this stuff," Alice continued. "She put all of you in the video I submitted with my application and made one for your hottie. It got us on the show, didn't it?"

For better or worse, it certainly had.

That *worse* part came to fruition pretty fast as the back door banged.

"I'm on fucking *Ghost House*?" Liam bellowed from her apartment in the back of the building. "Natalie! Where are you? What did you do?"

"Oh, good. He got the mail." Alice grinned.

Chapter Ten

"NATALIE..." LIAM'S VOICE WAS LOW AND measured as he faced her head-on. Eerily calm, which somehow seemed much more menacing than if he'd been yelling.

He held up his cell phone, ignoring the audience of both living and dead surrounding them.

"Why do I have an email saying, 'Congratulations, you've been chosen as a cast member for *Ghost House*!'?"

"I didn't do it. I swear." Natalie held up both palms defensively against the waves of doubt and suspicion radiating off Liam.

"Alice submitted for you," Harper jumped in, backing Natalie up, for which she was immensely grateful.

It was pretty perfect as far as alibis went. There was no way Liam would be mad at Alice. How could he be? She was old—double his age, at least. And tiny—almost half his size.

And, conveniently, it was the truth.

Most importantly, that little detail knocked the wind right out of Liam's sails. He drew in a breath and let it out slowly. Natalie had no doubt he was counting to ten to regain his cool.

Finally he said, in a tone that left no room for argument, "I'm not doing it."

"Okay. I understand," Natalie jumped in before Alice tried to convince him. "I'm honestly not sure I can even do it. Who's going to watch the store? I really can't just close for however long they'll need the cast in Utica. All the big book releases hit this time of year."

As much as she'd love to be there in Madame Letisha's face proving her a fraud, business was business. This was her livelihood.

"You won't have to close. I've got you covered," Harper said with a smile.

Before Natalie could question how, Jules burst through the door with Taco the spoiled chihuahua in his own little basket.

Jules put Taco's basket on the ground and the dog skittered across the floor, sniffing his way across the store, probably in search of Mr. Darcy. The antisocial cat had somehow formed a friendship with the overly friendly dog.

"I can't believe you got on the show," Jules began, channeling all of her college co-ed enthusiasm. "I'm so jealous I couldn't apply because of classes. But don't worry. Between Shalene and me we've got the shop fully covered."

"Who?" Natalie asked.

"Shalene is Stone's cousin. Agnes hired her to watch her house before I moved in," Harper supplied. "She's very reliable and so sweet."

"And she graduated college this year so she's available. She works at the Morgan's farm stand all the time—since she was a kid—but she said they can spare her when she needs to be here. And she knows how to use your point-of-sale system. They use the same one at the farm stand," Jules reported excitedly.

Natalie watched her life spin out of control. Or more accurately, it seemed her future was under the control of everyone else besides herself. All the decisions already made. And not one person had bothered to ask her opinion about any of it.

"Are you going to do it?" Liam finally asked.

At least he cared what she wanted. Or maybe he just wanted to know whether they'd be quitting the show together or if she'd succumb to the peer pressure and he'd be bowing out alone.

She glanced around the room and saw everyone's eyes on her, including Gabe's. She drew in a breath and let it out. "Yes. I'll do it."

"Yay!" Jules cheered in unison with Alice and Harper.

Gabe's lips twitched with a barely controlled smile. And Liam donned his typical expression of resolution.

He delivered a single nod and an, "Okay," which sounded like he'd expected that answer from her all along.

And in the middle of it all, the ghost bat decided to swoop back in through the front window and begin circling the room. That sent Taco, who could obviously see ghosts too, or at least ghosts of recently deceased bats, into a barking frenzy.

"Even Taco is excited," Jules said as the chihuahua began hopping up and down in a vain attempt to bite the bat flying yards above him. "Come on, boy. We have to go talk to Shalene and set up a work schedule."

As much as Natalie would be happy to have fewer people and a lot less noise around her right now, she had to stop Jules from running out to find Shalene. "Wait, Jules. I don't even know what days they'll need me yet."

"The schedule just came in another email," Harper said, looking at her cell. "We need to be in Utica Monday morning. They'll need us through the end of the live show Halloween night. And, oh—"

"Oh, what?" Natalie asked, suspicious at what had stopped Harper mid-sentence.

Harper glanced up. "There will be a camera crew here tomorrow morning at eight a.m. sharp to interview all of us."

Natalie drew in a breath as all of her fears came true. On camera interviews were not her favorite.

"Great," she said.

She glanced at Liam, who now wore a smirk as he said, "Have fun with that."

Chapter Eleven

Natalie stared at her reflection in the bathroom mirror beneath lighting that was so bad she probably should have gotten ready outside using the mirror in her car.

God only knew what her make-up would look like under the lights the crew would no doubt bring. She could only hope she didn't end up looking like a clown on camera.

This was the first time she'd worn a full face of make-up since—she thought about it—probably since the last time she'd been interviewed on camera by Lucy Sunshine on WBNG News. When she'd made a complete fool of herself.

In her defense, that time she had been surrounded

by dozens of extremely distracting ghosts who didn't understand the meaning of *personal space*.

She could only hope to do better this time. With a sigh, she turned off the switch for the crappy bathroom light fixture and headed toward the kitchen and the blissful aroma of fresh coffee.

Liam glanced up when she entered the room and shook his head. "I knew Harper would talk you into doing this thing."

She narrowed her eyes at him and walked to the coffee maker. "*You look very nice today, Natalie.* Oh, thank you, Liam. How sweet of you to notice," she said, holding the fictional conversation between them with herself.

His chair scraped across the floor and his arms came around her. With his hard body pressed against her back, he leaned his chin on her shoulder.

"You don't look *nice*. You look smoking hot. In fact, why haven't you ever worn this tight little skirt and sweater combo before?" he asked, his hands giving her hips a squeeze as he pulled her back tighter against him.

"Because these are my old work clothes from when I had to dress up every day." She gave a shudder as she remembered how much she hated that corporate job and how exorbitant her rent was so she could live in the city because of that job she hated.

"Well, maybe you can just wear it for me." His voice was low, husky, as he snuggled her neck.

"And maybe you're going to have to put a lid on your libido because the crew is going to be here any minute."

He groaned and released his hold on her. She took the opportunity to turn and face him, coffee mug in hand. "You're going to be there during the interview— Shit!"

She ducked as the damn bat swooped above her head. Then cursed again, ignoring Liam's frown as she glanced down at her sweater to see if the coffee that had sloshed out of her mug hit her or just the floor. Luckily, the liquid had missed her.

Annoyed at the world, she set down the mug, grabbed a paper towel and said, "And by the way, we have a ghost bat. That one from the other night must have died."

"Really? Cool."

She glared at Liam. "No. Not cool. If I can't keep myself from ducking every time it flies at my head they're going to lock me up."

Liam bobbed his head to the side. "At least then you wouldn't have to do the show."

"Ha-ha." She scowled. "And maybe I *want* to do the show."

"Do you?" he asked.

She considered that a moment, pawing through a mishmash of feelings. "Yeah. I think I do."

"Even though it could expose you?"

"Not gonna happen." Natalie shook her head, confident she could do both—expose Madame Letisha and *not* expose herself.

"We'll see." Liam lifted one brow along with his cup of coffee.

"Yes, we will," she declared—just as the banging on the front door threw her into a renewed sense of panic.

"Camera crew is here," Liam said with a grin.

"Yeah, great. Thanks." She paused before heading toward the front. "You'll be there with me?"

"Of course." He leaned in and dropped a quick kiss on her cheek then pulled back with a grin. "I still have to tell them I quit."

Chapter Twelve

"Doctor Walsh, tell us how you and Natalie met—"

"Liam is fine, and I'm not sure why I'm here. I told you I'm not doing the show."

"Yes, you did. But you're an important part of the story in connection to Natalie so if you could tell us how it was that you two met." The producer smiled at Liam who let out a soft huff.

"She stepped in a puddle that contained a downed live wire and got—" He glanced at Natalie as if he was reluctant to put into words what had happened. "Electrocuted."

"It's okay. You can say it," Natalie said to him before turning back to look at the producer... and then the camera. "I was dead. My heart stopped for three and a half minutes—there's video and everything—and Liam started it again. He's a real-life hero."

Natalie reached out and squeezed Liam's hand, who rolled his eyes. "It's nothing anyone else wouldn't have done."

"You were the only one there, so... No one else was coming to save me," Natalie pointed out.

"Jules was there to take the cell phone video. She could have performed CPR."

"I don't think so—"

"So you saved her life," the producer prompted, interrupting the on-camera bickering between Natalie and Liam.

"He did," Natalie said, staring at the camera.

"Miss Chase, if you could avoid looking directly at the camera, please."

Natalie cut her gaze to the producer. "Of course." But then found it was impossible to not glance at the camera again. It was like an irresistible urge now that she'd been told not to do it.

"I said *don't* look at the camera," the producer reminded.

"Sorry. I'm really horrible at this." Natalie cringed.

Hopefully they wouldn't pull up that WBNG footage and see exactly how horrible.

"You're doing fine. So that was how you two met?"

"Well, not exactly. We kind of met at the bar right before then," Natalie began. "He was there alone eating dinner and I was with my two friends having margaritas and he was of course the topic of conversation."

"Why was that?"

"He was new in town. And there were the rumors."

"What rumors were those?"

"That he was a serial killer... He wasn't, of course, but he kept to himself so much. And then there were the bodies..."

"You had to tell them that," Liam grumbled beside her.

"It's fine. I'm sure they'll edit it out," she whispered.

"I'm sure they *won't* and you do know whispering doesn't work when you're wearing a microphone. Right?" Liam asked, brows raised.

Natalie glanced down at the mic pinned to her collar and then at the ecstatic looking crew and said, "Oh. Oops."

"Ms. Mudd. Can you tell us about when you first became aware of Doctor William Walsh moving to town?"

"Doctor McHottie? Oh, sure. Everyone else thought he was a serial killer, because of the bodies. But I never really bought into that theory."

"Why not?"

"He didn't look the part. Didn't have those crazy eyes. You know, like Charles Manson had. I met him once at a party."

"Doctor Walsh?"

"No. Charles Manson. I could tell right away he was one to steer clear of."

"So back to the doctor..."

"Oh, yeah. So I figured he was probably doing wet work for the government. Black ops. Assassinations. Hit man type stuff, you know? He just looked the part. The handsome leading man action movie type. Like James Bond. Now *him* I've never met but I'd sure like to."

"Doctor Walsh—"

"Liam."

"Liam, can you tell us about the bodies?"

"Jeezus— There's nothing to tell. I'm a researcher. I've done work with cadavers...acquired legally and officially through the Albany Medical College Anatomical Gift Program."

"What kind of research are you currently working on with your cadavers?"

"You really want to hear about this?"

"Definitely."

"Okay. Until very recently the military believed low level blasts to be harmless. But through recent studies on the brains of troops whose MOS exposed them to repeated low-level blasts during training across a twenty-year career, a definite connection can now be drawn between the cognitive issues reported by the subjects while alive and an unusual pattern of brain damage pervasive in all of those same subjects after their death—by suicide. And it wasn't, as originally assumed, CTE—"

"CTE?"

"Chronic traumatic encephalopathy—like is found in football players. But it wasn't. Six out of eight samples of brain tissue taken from Navy SEALs who'd all died by suicide revealed a microscopic pattern of brain damage. Interface astroglial scarring—scar tissue not found in civilians—unique in the brains of troops and caused by repeated blast waves. And two of the eight displayed a severe mutation to the astrocytes caused by the vacuum that every blast creates in the brain. It literally explodes the brain liquid causing cavitation... Anyway, my grant is allowing me to study a wider sample of brain tissue to further support the initial study. Now that we know the problem, we can find solutions that will lead to safer training practices and a reduction in veteran suicides. Not to mention accurate diagnosis and a new understanding of these affected troops while they're alive."

"So your research is to study the brains of military personnel."

"At the most basic level, yes."

"Can we get a tour of your lab?"

"No."

"Miss Lowinsky—"

"Actually, could we use Harper Lowry on camera? That's my pen name. It's the name I use publicly."

"Of course. Can you tell us how you came to suspect your house was haunted?"

"It's actually my Great Aunt Agnes's house but I've lived there with her for a while now. And recently I heard footsteps and a voice. The same voice that Liam

—Doctor Walsh—recorded on the equipment he brought into our house."

"Doctor Walsh. Let's switch gears."

"Please do."

"It's my understanding you are the one who recorded the voice of what appears to be a spirit inside Miss Lowry's residence."

"Um. Uh. Yes. I guess I did."

"And what do you think about it?"

"About what?"

"The voice you recorded. As a researcher you look for evidence to prove a hypothesis or theory. Would you agree with that statement?"

"Yes."

"Do you consider the voice recording proof of the existence of ghosts and the theory that they do indeed want to communicate with us?"

"Uh..."

"Let me repeat the question. Do you, Dr. Walsh, believe in the existence of ghosts?"

"Um..."

"Doctor—

"Yes. I heard you. And yes. Based on the evidence,

it would appear that the existence of ghosts is possible and that some are capable of communicating with the living."

"Go, McHottie! Do you think this means he'll do the show?"

"Shh. Alice. They're recording."

"Natalie, would you agree with your fiancé?"

"My fiancé— Oh. No. Liam's not my fiancé. Harper's the one engaged. To Stone. Liam and I are just... dating."

"I stand corrected. Then would you say you agree with Liam that ghosts exist?"

"Yes?"

"Is that a question, Natalie? Are you uncertain about your answer or about the existence of spirits?"

"Um... No..."

"Miss Chase, in your opinion, definitively, do ghosts exist?"

"She's not going to say it."

"Hush up, Gabe. She'll say it."

"You want to put some money down on that? A little friendly wager. Harriet? Gabe?"

"Shut up, Ricky."

"Seriously, Rick. You know I haven't had money in my hand since the nineteen-seventies when I died. What an absolutely silly proposition."

"It's just an expression. Jeez. You two need to lighten up."

Natalie drew in a breath, tuned out the ghost chatter, raised her gaze to meet that of the producer and said, "One hundred percent, ghosts do exist and are both willing and able of communicating with the living."

"And have you ever personally communicated with a spirit?"

The dead silence in the room, even from the three ghosts assembled, had Natalie swallowing hard. Finally, she nodded.

"A verbal answer if you could, please, Miss Chase."

She licked her lips, though it didn't do much good since her mouth felt as dry as cotton, and said, "Yes."

"Whoop! Good on you, doll."

"About damn time. Jeez."

"Stop grumbling, Gabe. I told you two gentlemen she'd do it."

"You should've taken that bet."

Natalie would have liked to watch the producer's face for a reaction to her statement, and she would have if the ghost bat hadn't swooped back inside and straight at her head.

With a yip she couldn't control, Natalie ducked and threw her hands up over her face.

"Are you all right, Miss Chase?"

"Mm-hm. Fine. Just dodging a mosquito. I hate those things." She flapped her hand around her head again for effect.

The producer's brows rose high.

Yup. They already thought she was looney-tunes. And since there was probably nothing she could do to change that, she might as well lean into it.

In for a penny, in for a pound.

"And while we're on the subject of communing with the dead," Natalie began. "Madame Letisha is a liar..."

Chapter Thirteen

"You don't do anything halfway, do you?" Liam asked, arms crossed, judgmental brow cocked high.

Natalie slumped in one of the chairs in the meeting room. "Have you met me?"

That dark brow remained high. "Yes, I have. Yet in spite of that you still continue to surprise me."

"Surprise is good in a relationship. Keeps things fresh. Don't you think?"

"Depends on the surprise," Liam grumbled. "You couldn't just say what I did? That based on the evidence on the recording it's possible ghosts were real. Instead you had to go off and declare that not only do you speak to them but that Letisha only pretends to."

"I thought you all wanted me to confess."

"*You all?* I can't speak for Gabe but I for one only wanted you to confess to Harper and Stone. Not the entire viewership of the Paranormal Channel."

Speaking of the Paranormal Channel—the crew had packed up and left after having gotten all they needed. Plus more than they'd probably hoped for after Natalie had spilled more than she'd intended to.

The ghosts had left right after the crew. They went off to report on the morning's happenings to the others.

And after congratulating her on an amazing *performance* for the producer and cameras, Harper and Alice had both rushed off to pack since apparently they all had to be in Utica Monday.

That was the most ironic part of this whole thing. Now that she'd actually told the truth, Harper and Alice assumed it was an act.

It was... a lot. It wasn't even ten in the morning yet and Natalie was completely exhausted already.

"So what now?" Liam asked, leaning against the arm of the chair in which she sat.

Her eyes drifted closed momentarily as he began to work the tension out of her shoulders with those magic hands of his.

"Now I have to unlock the front door." It was time. There was no denying that as the grandfather clock began to chime for the ten o'clock hour.

"I'm not talking about the shop. I'm talking about the confession," Liam said.

She let out a laugh. "You saw their faces. Nobody believed me. The show's crew thinks I'm a nut. And our friends just think I'm an amazing actress."

But at least the ghosts—who seemed to have lost the capability of accurately reading human reactions— were happy about her confession. Now all she had to deal with was the reaction of the living world.

Natalie groaned. "They're going to make me look like a lunatic in editing."

She'd watched enough reality television to know how it worked. Very early on the producers chose which role each cast member would fill. She'd be positioned as the amateur nutcase who thought she could speak to ghosts while claiming a well-known professional medium could not.

Liam sniffed out a laugh. "That won't take much editing."

She slapped at his leg. "Hey, you admitted on camera to hearing Gabe too."

"I did. With the existence of that recording you made of Gabe, I didn't have much choice, did I? I can only hope that doesn't come back to bite me in the ass in the science community. I'll just have to claim I was forced into that admission based on the empirical evidence. And let's remember I didn't do it quite as enthusiastically as you. You know, you could just have Gabe talk in front of the cameras and crew. Once everyone hears him, they won't be able to question your sanity."

"I could have had Gabe speak today, except that Millie's not here. She's still in Sharon Springs visiting her family. And I don't know if Gabe and Millie can travel as far as the theater." Natalie slumped lower with a renewed wave of defeat.

"Why can't they? Isn't Utica about as far from here as Sharon Springs?"

"Is it? I don't know." Excitement began to build.

Liam nodded. "I looked into taking a train from the station there once. Both towns are about an hour and a half drive... I don't know how long that would be converted to ghost travel time, but the distance is probably about the same."

Natalie sagged again. "But what if Millie can travel to Sharon Springs because she has relatives buried there? Just like how Train Track Tim can visit Afton because his cousin is there."

"Tim's gone away too? These ghosts do more traveling than I do," Liam grumbled.

"Liam. Focus. The point is maybe my ghosts won't be able to go to Utica if they have no connection to there."

"Do you know that for certain?"

"No. Nobody knows anything about this for *certain*. Not even the ghosts. There's no rule book. We're all just guessing here."

"Well, that's real scientific." He rolled his eyes.

"Spoken like a true scientist." She scowled.

That's what she got for dating a doctor.

She looked up at him above her. "You could come and be there with me."

"Nope."

"Liam—"

"Natalie, I love you, but public humiliation on a major television network that could cost me my professional reputation, my career, my grant and my life's work is where I draw the line."

"What about my reputation and my work?" she asked.

"Babe, being known as the kooky ghost lady will only increase business. The shop will end up being a tourist destination with you as the main attraction. Believe me. You'll be fine."

She scowled again, hating that he was probably right. And not just because she hated when he was right, but more because the scenario he'd just described sounded like a living hell.

Chapter Fourteen

"Is there anything I can do to convince you to come with us?" Natalie tipped her chin down and her eyes up as she stared seductively at Liam.

Since he smiled—the kind of smile that led to a laugh and not to the bedroom—she guessed she'd failed at her seduction.

"Not a thing. Nice try though, babe. I love you. Be good." He wrapped her in a hug before releasing her.

"Not sure what trouble I could get into in Utica with Alice as a chaperone but okay, I'll be good."

"I was talking more about your interactions with Madame Letisha. I don't want to have to drive up there to bail you out of jail."

She let out a snort. "I won't end up in jail. She's the one who should be in jail."

"Save that piss and vinegar for Letisha. Now get. Alice and Harper are standing by your car with suitcases." Liam lifted a chin toward the front window.

"Suitcases?" Natalie spun to look, her one oversized tote bag in her hand. "What did they pack?"

"I don't know but it looks like they're ready to go."

She turned back. "Jules's friend Shalene should be here by ten to open. She's Stone's cousin."

"I know. And you left Agnes's number in case of emergency and Stone's number in case his cousin doesn't show. I got it. I've had more responsibility on my shoulders over the years than making sure someone opens the shop by ten. I promise you. It'll be fine."

Natalie drew in a breath and let it out, the dread riding her hard. She didn't want to go. She missed home already and she hadn't left yet. The shop, the ghosts, Liam... even the damn antisocial cat.

Liam pinned her with his gaze. "It's only five days."

She scowled.

He ran his hands up and down her arms. "And I'm just a phone call away."

"A phone call and an hour and a half away, you mean."

"You wanted to do this," he reminded in his lecturer voice.

"That's helpful. Thank you." She felt the pout settle on her lips.

He cupped her face with both palms and kissed the pout away.

"I'll miss you, but you have to actually leave first so…" He turned her and walked her toward the door, opening it for them both when they got there.

Before she knew it she was on the sidewalk and surrounded by her two babbling travel companions.

Liam took the keys out of her hand and opened the trunk for Alice and Harper's luggage. Enough they could be circumnavigating the globe, by the looks of it.

"Call when you arrive."

"Will do, Doc. Right before they take our phones away." Alice delivered that news with a mock salute.

"Wait, what?" Natalie spun to face Alice.

"Didn't you read the rules?" Alice asked.

"They don't want the cast to have any contact with the outside world," Harper explained.

Natalie spun wide-eyed toward Liam. He gripped her shoulders and leaned his head toward hers. "It will be fine."

"Oh, good. You're still here." Gabe swooped in. "I thought I'd missed saying good luck."

"I don't want to go," she whispered as much to Gabe as to Liam.

"Little late for that, Nat. Didn't you sign a contract?" Gabe cocked up a brow high.

In a mirror move, so did Liam, but he didn't lecture her. He just kissed her mouth one more time, then opened the car door.

As she reluctantly sat in the driver's seat, Liam said, "Do great. I'll be watching you."

"Me too," Gabe called from behind Liam. "But I hope he watches on the television at your place instead of on his laptop in the lab. Tell him that, Nat."

Oh, God. Just what she needed. Reminders that the world would be watching her on camera—her least favorite place to be.

But she did manage to say, "Watch on the television in my apartment, okay? In case someone wanted to watch with you."

"Who would be watching—oh. Yeah. Okay. Will do," Liam agreed as realization hit.

"Thank you." Gabe grinned.

"This is so exciting!" Harper squealed from the front seat as Alice climbed into the back.

"If we ever get there it will be," Alice sniped, leaning forward between the seats.

"I guess I'd better go." Natalie raised her gaze to Liam's. If he asked her to stay, she would. She'd break that contract and send Harper and Alice on their merry way.

What Liam said instead was, "Letisha's waiting. Go get her."

And that was the exact perfect thing to get her motivated.

"We will," Harper said, leaning low to answer Liam.

"Next stop, Utica! Or maybe that rest stop on the way because I'm gonna have to go before then," Alice informed them, coaxing a laugh from Natalie.

"All right. We're going," she said and with one more wistful look at Liam, shifted the car into drive.

"Can I turn on the radio? Would you mind?" Harper asked.

"How about turning on the heat? A girl could freeze to death back here," Alice added.

They hadn't even turned onto Main Street yet but Natalie could already see how this drive was going to go.

She swung onto Main Street, heading in the direction of the entrance to the highway that would—for better or worse—take them to Utica for what could be the biggest mistake of her life.

"Feel free to turn on the radio. And Alice, don't you have your own heat controls back there?" Natalie glanced in the rearview mirror to look at Alice. "Right there facing you in the center console."

When she brought her gaze back to the road, it was to see a full-sized horse, complete with a rider coming directly at them at full speed dead center in the middle of the street.

She screeched, swerving to avoid the animal. The car bumped up on the curb, then back off again as she overcorrected to avoid crashing through the iron rail fencing of the cemetery.

"Jeez, doll! Where are you going?" Ricky shouted from behind the fence.

But she couldn't deal with him as she slammed on the brakes, rocking the car to a stop along the curb.

She spun to look where the horse and rider had gone, just in time to see the animal gallop right through a UPS truck.

Ghost horse. Sybil.

The ghosts had told her about this. But holy crap, hearing about it was one thing. Coming against it, face-to-face at full speed, was quite another.

Heart pounding, Natalie finally turned to face her passengers. "Everyone all right?"

Harper, one hand still gripping the handle on the roof while the other braced on the dash stared at her.

"I'm in one piece, miraculously. If I knew you were

such a bad driver I would have offered to drive. It would have been safer, and the idiots at DMV took my license away last year," Alice grumbled as she reached to put on the seat belt she hadn't been wearing.

"Sorry. I'm fine. I just saw an animal."

"Death by squirrel. That's not how I wanna go out so just hit the damn thing next time and keep going, will ya?" Alice suggested.

"Yeah. I know. Sorry. It won't happen again." Heart pounding, Natalie flipped on her blinker, checked both mirrors and eased carefully into the lane.

"Good luck on the show, doll!" Ricky called from the cemetery amid what had become a gathering crowd of local spirits, most of whom she recognized.

The reminder that she was leaving those she knew and heading to face new spirits in a new place caused a twisting in her chest. Part dread. Part fear. Part plain old nostalgia to be leaving what she'd come to think of as *her* ghosts. Some of them friends.

"Break a leg!" Amanda yelled from the sidewalk.

"Don't embarrass us. Or yourself," Bob, standing next to his wife, yelled.

"Oh, for fuck's sake, Bob. Be nice!" Amanda slapped her husband in the arm.

Natalie pursed her lips to resist reacting to the voices the others couldn't hear.

She forced her attention back to the road and accelerated away from the cemetery and toward the highway that would take her away from Mudville on this fateful road trip.

If the rest of the week continued like this, it was going to be one hell of a ride...

Chapter Fifteen

"THIS IS THE EXIT. UTICA! GIVE ME McHottie's cell number and I'll text him for you. Tell him we're here," Alice offered.

Natalie wasn't certain of much right now, but she did know the last thing Liam would want was Alice having his cell number. If anyone in Mudville would abuse that privilege it would be the octogenarian who still acted like a teenager most days.

"Thanks, Alice. I'll text him after we get there and I park the car."

"I just messaged Stone and Agnes that we're almost there. They'll pass along the update to Liam and Jules and everyone else back home who's interested."

Natalie nodded, thinking the whole town was likely interested.

Them getting on this show was the most exciting thing to happen in Mudville since Taco dug up that human bone in the shop's backyard.

Over the past few days, walk-in business had doubled. Just like it had then after the discovery of the bone. It seemed like everyone stopped by to ask questions or get an update. Or just to be able to say they'd been in the shop that was the subject of the most exciting recent gossip.

And Natalie had left it in the hands of Stone's cousin whom she'd met once yesterday, and Jules, her college freshman part-time employee.

Pushing that fear aside, she moved onto the next worry that had occupied her mind for most of the ride. While Alice had been dictating the radio station selection from the backseat, and Harper had spent most of the ride trying to keep Alice happy, Natalie's mind spun with thoughts about what was to come.

How the hell was this ghost show going to play out now that she'd openly declared war with Letisha by calling her a fraud during her cast interview?

As the theater came into view, she figured she'd know soon enough. She slowed to a crawl now that she was in the town, then spotted the parking lot for the theater and swung the car in.

Knowing her vehicle was so close, a means of escape should she need it, made her feel momentarily better—until she realized the producers could easily demand she hand over her car key along with her cell phone.

She wished she'd listened to Liam and hid a spare car key in one of those magnetic hide-a-key things like he'd suggested.

Of course, she'd never gotten around to it, a fact she regretted immensely right now. She had a feeling that was going to be the first of many regrets this week.

Cutting the engine, she turned to Harper. "This is it."

"I know," Harper squealed. "It's so exciting!"

"Yeah. Exciting," Natalie echoed with far less enthusiasm. "I'm just going to text Liam."

"Pop the trunk. We got bags to unload," Alice demanded, as if either of them was going to let the old lady lift anything heavy.

Natalie did as told, figuring they'd wrestle over the bags later. She popped the trunk then typed out a quick text.

We're here. Miss you already!

She hit send and waited, but he didn't get back to her.

There were no telltale bubbles to indicate he was typing a message either.

He was probably deep into his research with the cell on silent, as usual. Only this time she couldn't walk next door to the lab to see him.

Fighting back the panic that knowledge caused, she drew in a breath.

It was going to be okay.

God, how she hoped it was going to be okay.

She pocketed the cell, missing the device already too even though it hadn't been confiscated as yet, and got out of the car.

"You'd think they'd send out a valet. Don't they know three fashionable women are going to have a lot of luggage?" Alice said, standing next to the bags of various sizes and shapes.

Natalie wasn't sure she or Alice qualified as *fashionable*.

Harper did, in black leggings, knee-high riding boots and a Burberry plaid cape over a black turtleneck, all of which she'd bragged she'd procured at Red's Resale shop for pennies on the dollar compared to what it was all worth.

But not Natalie, in what was probably out of style

by now skinny jeans topped with a plain cream-colored oversized sweater and knock-off camel-colored Ugg boots. Nor Alice, in her hot pink jogging pants with a white turtleneck under a matching pink zip-up sweatshirt and bright white slip-on sneakers. Yeah. They weren't winning any fashion awards today.

Natalie glanced toward the building, about to assure Alice that she and Harper could handle the baggage, when she spotted a young man heading their direction. "It's okay, Alice. I see someone coming. I bet he's here to help us."

"I don't see nobody," Alice said.

"Did you remember to pack your glasses, Alice?" Harper asked, arranging her smaller bag so it set atop her larger roller suitcase.

"I don't need no stinking glasses to know there ain't nobody coming. I only use glasses for reading, not for distance," Alice sniped back.

Harper turned, shading her eyes as she peered toward the building too. "Actually, I don't see anyone either. Where did you see someone, Natalie?"

Uh, oh. No. Could it be? Already?

Heart racing, Natalie moved around the car and then stopped as the young man got closer.

She could see the dark bruising around his deeply sunken eyes. The yellow pallor to his skin. And the clincher, what really sold the fact this boy might not be alive, was his uniform. Unless the theater dressed their employees in historical outfits, this was a ghost.

A new ghost. A stranger to her. Not one of her ghosts. And she didn't know if he was friendly or not.

He could just as easily be a psychopath who'd murdered his way through 1920s chorus girls until he succumbed to... whatever it was that killed him. Now he was cursed to haunt the theater forever. Torturing both the living and the dead, and especially the living who could see the dead.

Natalie yanked her gaze away from the specter moving closer. She couldn't let him realize she could see him. At least until she got the lay of the land. Figured out the temper of these spirits and knew it was safe to communicate.

That time in the tunnels at the prohibition-era distillery when she met that bootlegger ghost at least she had Liam with her. Same with the two ghosts in their hotel room on that trip. And in Mudville, Gabe was there, always playing interference, remaining between her and the spirit community. Protecting her.

But here. Here she was all on her own.

She spun away from the building, forcing her focus to remain on Harper, or Alice, or the mound of luggage. Anywhere except on the ghost.

Keeping her voice as low as she thought she could for Alice to be able to hear, she said, "I, uh, saw someone but I lost sight of them again... in the glare of the sun. They probably went back inside. That's fine. We can handle it. Alice, you just grab your purse and Harper and I can handle the rest."

And so it had begun. The first of what would no doubt be many and growingly intricate lies.

This was going to be a week filled with her tripping up around the spirits and then lying creatively to the livings about it.

She was going to have to lie like she'd never lied before. And do it convincingly too because she needed the producers to believe in her—in her honesty, in her integrity—if she wanted to expose Letisha as a fraud.

But she also had to keep her friends from learning the truth—that she wasn't just pretending to see ghosts to expose Letisha.

And to do that she needed to stop slipping up. Swerving to avoid the ghost horse, announcing the ghost usher coming to help them—that all had to stop.

Maybe she needed to fake laryngitis and stop talking all together because things were about to get really complicated really fast.

"You must be Natalie, Harper and Alice from Mudville. I'm Samantha Carr—you can call me Sam. I'm the producer on this project. Welcome to *Halloween Ghost Challenge*!"

"I would have taken help with the luggage over this bubbly broad's *welcome*," Alice mumbled behind Natalie.

Harper subtly shushed Alice before taking a step forward, arm extended. "Harper Lowry. A pleasure to meet you, Sam. We're all thrilled to be here representing Mudville."

As Sam accepted the handshake it was obvious Harper had engaged *professional mode*. It was a good thing she'd stepped up to the plate as ad hoc Mudville ambassador. Natalie wasn't sure she had the mental bandwidth to deal with everything happening around her.

"But I thought the show was called *Ghost House*," Harper pointed out.

Sam pressed her lips together and nodded. "It was, until the hit movie of the year released last week and it, we discovered, contains a show called *Ghost House*."

"So the fictional show within a movie was named the same thing as your actual show." Harper nodded. "Understood. Don't want a lawsuit."

"No, we do not," Sam agreed.

Meanwhile, Natalie found herself holding her breath as the gathering press of ghosts closed in on them. The closeness proving those spirits trapped here on earth in the afterlife had lost the ability to respect the personal space of the living. The show's crew seemed to suffer from the same affliction as one cameraman pushed in close enough Natalie could read the name printed on the ID badge that hung by a lanyard around his neck—*Jake Romano*.

She resisted the urge even though she really wanted to channel Harper and say, *Nice to meet you, Jake... Now get out of my face.*

But cameras were all part of what she'd signed up for, so Natalie forced a tight-lipped smile for the camera and tried not to react when a child ran directly at her, curls bouncing. The stage make-up and the perfect child-sized version of an adult turn of the century dress made the girl look like a miniature grown-up.

The illusion only added to make Natalie's first child ghostly encounter even more disturbing.

What had this girl died from and why hadn't she moved on? Natalie wondered that as she stoically held still, even as the girl reached out one tiny ghostly hand and petted Natalie's boots.

"Ooo. I like these," the girl cooed. "They're soft."

"Ugh, Clara. No. Just no. Girl, let Bobby tell you something. As one of the most acclaimed costume designers of my time, no woman who Bobby LaRue dressed would leave looking like an outdoorsman like this one here." Bobby, who apparently liked to refer to himself in the third person, waved a hand in Natalie's direction as he lectured the girl ghost about fashion.

"The sweater is much too baggy but maybe not irredeemable," he continued. "Picture this same outfit but with a nice white patent-leather boot with a high chunky heel. I do like her friend's outfit though. Very chic but also casual. Those high black boots. Perfection."

Bobby LaRue, flamboyant to the bone, appeared every bit the quintessential nineteen-seventies costume designer as he delivered a chef's kiss into the air while the girl continued to stroke Natalie's boots.

With a creepy tingling running up her spine and her foot getting cold from the icy touch of the child ghost's attention, Natalie stood frozen in place pointedly not looking at either ghost.

Meanwhile, oblivious to Natalie's situation, Sam the producer waved a twenty-something dark-haired man over to where they stood. "We have refreshments and a get to know each other gathering for the cast and crew starting in a bit. But first, we have to take care of business. Aiden here is the show's tech guy. He'll be collecting your cell phones for the duration of filming. But don't worry. We'll keep them locked up safe."

That was just one more thing that had Natalie ready to bolt. Besides the cameras and the ghosts in her face—a week without any way to contact home was terrifying.

She couldn't check on the shop. Wouldn't be able to hear Liam's voice when she needed to—like right now. And if someone needed to reach her, they wouldn't be able to.

"What if there's an emergency at home?" Natalie asked, still clutching her cell so tightly she was starting to lose feeling in her fingers.

"That's why we provided an email address and

phone number in your paperwork. If there is an emergency, your loved ones can contact us and we'll get you." Sam smiled as if Aiden the tech guy wasn't about to take away the only security blanket Natalie had left.

"Sounds good. No problem at all!" Alice said and dramatically dropped her cell phone into Aiden's bag with a flourish, before she turned to Natalie and Harper and delivered an open-mouthed, exaggerated wink.

What in the hell was that all about?

Natalie would have asked except Aiden wasn't done with them yet.

"We're going to set you up with your microphones now. We want to capture every moment, every word, every sound while you're here. Day and night." Sam smiled again, as if she hadn't just announced an absolutely horrific scenario. "Okay?"

Every moment. Every word. Every sound.

"Sounds good," Harper said as Aiden outfitted her with her microphone.

"Yeah. Sounds great," Natalie said, hoping Aiden's sound system didn't pick up her sarcasm.

"Even in the toilet?" Alice asked leaning in before she elbowed Natalie in the side. "Guess I'm glad I packed that Gas-X and Pepto, eh? Along with a few other things." Alice winked again.

Natalie managed a nod as Aiden walked right through Bobby. The ghost gave an exaggerated shudder, before fluttering his hand to fan his face as he said, "Woo. I just love when the hot ones walk through me."

Aiden wasn't unaffected himself. She saw the tremor of a chill run through him as well. He frowned, but the unseen ghostly encounter didn't stop him from coming at her with her microphone.

He did mumble, "Hope they turn the heat up in here."

Natalie smothered a snort. She knew from personal experience turning up the heat didn't help when a ghost decided to walk through a living.

She nodded in agreement with him anyway. "Let's hope."

While she was at it, she could hope the half dozen —and growing—ghosts surrounding them never figured out that she could see and hear them.

Chapter Seventeen

Natalie might as well have been at this get to know you party naked. That's how she felt without her cell phone while being many, many miles away from her boyfriend and her ghosts.

Thank goodness Harper, and even Alice, were there. Natalie stayed glued to them as they entered the lobby of the theater.

The large space was appointed with ornate architectural details which Natalie—no expert—assumed were appropriate to the era in which it was built.

The ornate decor, heavy with gold and filigree, was dominated by a sweeping grand central staircase that led to the upper level. While the lower level had been set-up with all the trappings of a cocktail party—if cocktail parties had multiple camera crews.

"Ooo. Shrimp." With that exclamation, Alice motored off toward the buffet table.

Harper watched her go. "Should we follow her?"

"How much trouble can she get into?" Natalie asked but reevaluated that assumption when she saw Alice mound more shrimp than could possibly fit onto the tiny plate clutched in her arthritic fingers.

"I guess her consuming too much shrimp is better than too much alcohol," Harper commented.

"With Alice, it's more likely to be shrooms or pot we need to watch out for." Natalie laughed.

Harper chuckled. "That's the truth. You think she brought any with her?"

"God, I hope not." Natalie shook her head.

She had enough to deal with without having to babysit Alice. Or Harper. Or getting accidentally drugged herself from unknowingly drinking some of Alice's signature tea or lemonade spiked with one drug or another.

Although now Alice had turned to cannabis gummies, formulated with melatonin and lavender to help with sleep. They'd heard all about it on the long drive and about how she couldn't sleep without them so there was a good chance there were some smuggled here in that big suitcase of hers.

That might not be a bad thing. Alice's pot gummies might be the only thing that would allow Natalie to sleep this week. If she could allow herself to sleep here. She wasn't sure how she felt about being even a little incapacitated amid a strange ghost population now that she knew the cast would be sleeping here. In the theater.

Before the party, they'd gotten a look at their rooms for the duration of the show.

Thank goodness there were dressing rooms for the performers' use, and incorporated into those were bathrooms with showers. Even so, a cast of eight, living together, eating together, sleeping together, here in the theater for a week—it was going to be interesting.

She, Harper and Alice had been put together in one of the multiple dressing rooms on site. The room was clean and white, brightly lined with mirrors, and now also with three roll-away beds. It was apparently one of the chorus dressing rooms and located on the mezzanine level of the theater.

Living here in the theater, day and night, made her little apartment in the back of the shop in the historic train depot seem luxurious in comparison.

The cohabitation with the other cast members didn't bother Natalie much. Mainly because she was more concerned with the spirit population of the theater.

She might never get the image of the female spirit laid out on one of the beds, apparently napping, until one of the crew tossed Alice's suitcase right on top of her. The spirit's blood-curdling scream still echoed through her mind.

"I suppose we should mingle with the rest of the cast and get to know the crew better," Harper said.

"I suppose," Natalie agreed, but she barely comprehended what she was agreeing to because one hundred percent of her focus was drawn to the party's newest arrival.

Making a grand entrance that was no doubt intended to catch the attention of every being in the room—living and dead—the woman who swept down the staircase looked like she was ready for her close-up. No doubt she was, draped in ethereal clothing made of a fabric that seemed somehow luminescent as it shone with gold and all the colors of the rainbow depending on how it caught the light.

Madame Letisha.

None of the other cast members or crew had felt

the need to use the grand staircase. They'd used the elevator to come down from the upper level.

Natalie barely contained the obscenity-laced commentary that ran through her head and almost escaped out her mouth. The only reason it didn't come out was because when she spun to Harper, she saw the wire and microphone and remembered everything they said would be captured and possibly used on the show.

She didn't need to say anything anyway.

Harper's gaze was pinned to Letisha as she said low, "Look who's here. Wanna bet she isn't sharing a room? In fact, I bet she's in that single dressing room on the stage level labeled "Star" with its own private shower and toilet."

"On the stage level, you said?" Which would make it extra ridiculous Letisha had gone upstairs just to come back down.

Harper nodded. "It's marked on the map they gave us."

Map? Natalie should really have read the materials. But it didn't matter because she knew one thing for certain without any papers or maps—Letisha was all about image. And that would make it even more satisfying when they knocked her off her pedestal.

Alice, with her laden plate, wandered over.

"Coconut shrimp," she announced, holding one up between her two gnarly fingers. Then she tipped her head toward the staircase. "See who's trying to make a grand entrance? Boy, is she going to be fun to take down."

Maybe she and Alice were more alike than Natalie had realized.

Chapter Eighteen

A LOUD CLAPPING OF HANDS HAD NATALIE jumping.

"People! People! Gather round. Now that we're all here, it's time for introductions."

Natalie was too on edge, her nerves strung too tightly right now, for her to be able to deal with this overly energetic producer's method of getting the cast and crews' attention. But she supposed she'd better get used to it.

"First of all welcome to *Halloween Ghost Challenge*. I am your producer, Samantha Carr but--"

"*Please call me Sam,*" Natalie mumbled in perfect sync along with the producer's words.

Harper heard and let out a chuckle. Alice,

clustered close to the Mudville coalition, must have been too busy crunching on deep fried coconut shrimp to hear.

"Most of you have already met Aiden Kim when he wired you for sound. This guy here with the camera is Jake Romano. There are a few more of us you'll see around. Please remember we're invisible. So just ignore us."

"Easy for her to say," Natalie mumbled as Jake the not so invisible panned around the room with his ever-present camera.

"Now for the host of our show, Montgomery Tristane. He'll be here with us occasionally as kind of a master of ceremonies. Montgomery, if you could help us introduce the cast?" Sam asked.

"Of course," he said, with a sweeping bow.

Just then a clattering crash sounded, giving the whole group a start.

Natalie had jumped too, from the sheer loudness of the sound, but she assumed one of the crew must have dropped something metal.

Montgomery, on the other hand, cursed and clutched his hand to his heart. He looked around, then toward Sam, eyes wide. "Was that a ghost? Are they unhappy we're here disturbing them?"

"I think a caterer dropped a tray," said a fifty-something year old man with a sarcastic mocking lilt in his tone.

He wore glasses, khaki pants and a light blue button-down shirt that had been buttoned up way too high on his neck considering he wasn't wearing a tie.

"Doctor Oliver Finch," Sam prompted. When Montgomery didn't pick up on the cue, she said, "Your teleprompter is right there by the camera, Monty."

"Oh, yes. Of course." He cleared his throat, visibly donned his star persona and read in a voice somehow deeper than it had been a moment ago, "Doctor Oliver Finch, physicist. He will provide a more science-oriented analytical angle for any unexplained phenomenon or paranormal occurrences."

Looking slightly bored, like all of this was beneath him, Dr. Finch gave a single restrained nod in response to his introduction.

"Oh, he looks like he's gonna be a barrel of laughs," Alice commented, mouth full of partially chewed food.

Natalie silently agreed with Alice as she saw Harper next to her valiantly fighting a smile.

Montgomery continued, "The face of our next participant might seem slightly familiar to some of you. Please welcome Tiffany Collins, former child star of the hit sit com *Daddy Knows Best...Maybe!*"

A thirty-something year old woman, dressed from head-to-toe in what Natalie supposed the former star thought was an appropriate outfit but instead made her look like she was about to go to a disco, took a step forward and lifted one arm in a practiced wave.

Harper frowned. "Wow. Really? That's her? I would've never recognized her and I used to watch that show."

"Reality shows are where all the has-beens go to die. There and made-for-TV Christmas movies." Alice had stopped eating long enough to lean in and deliver that surprisingly on-point assessment of the current entertainment industry.

"Another face some of you might recognize if you're one of his twenty million followers, YouTube sensation Derek Simmons."

A guy with a mop of green-tipped blonde hair, baggy pants and a graphic T-shirt stepped forward with a bold wave and a loud, "Yeo!"

He looked barely old enough to legally drink, never mind old enough to have accumulated millions of followers.

What did he do to attract that much attention? Skateboarding? Snowboarding? Something Natalie had never done, she was sure. At her age, and while hanging around with Alice, the only board sport Natalie had hopes of doing would be shuffleboard.

"Next we have three women who say they've all had up close and personal ghostly encounters. From nearby Mudville, New York, Alice Mudd, Harper Lowinsky and Natalie Chase."

"Lowry. It's Harper *Lowry*," Harper corrected but it was doubtful anyone heard over the spattering of half-hearted applause of those in the lobby.

Alice bowed and Natalie resisted the urge to hide behind her hand. That was it. The world would hear she claimed to have *ghostly encounters*. There was no going back now.

During the lengthy introductions the ghosts had hung back along the edge of the gathering. They observed everything but were mostly quiet, which made it easier for Natalie to ignore them. At least mostly. But once Montgomery read that she, Harper and Alice had claimed to see ghosts, the spirits in the room began to stir and the volume of the ghostly chatter picked up.

"And now for our final two participants," Montgomery began. "She's a self-proclaimed fan girl of ghost shows, in particular the *Beyond the Veil* podcast, Megan Foster."

A shy woman raised one hand awkwardly as her eyes remained downcast. Then she leaned back into the shadows along the wall where she'd gone unnoticed by Natalie who'd been avoiding looking too closely at any figures standing along the periphery in the shadows, figuring they'd be ghosts.

Megan, self-proclaimed fan girl, was perhaps in her thirties and nondescript in every way. Medium height, mousy brown hair, a long dark-colored skirt and a sweater that was about one shade lighter. She didn't appear as if she got excited about anything... until Montgomery announced Madame Letisha's name.

"And finally, Madame Letisha, the woman who will lead our investigations this week. She's the host of *Beyond the Veil* as well as world renowned as a medium and clairvoyant."

Megan's wall flower shell fell away as she clapped her hands rapidly, drowning out the end of Montgomery's introduction.

She bounced up and down on her toes and showed more enthusiastic energy than Natalie thought the woman capable of.

Megan was still clapping for Letisha when Montgomery swept his arm to encompass them all and announced more loudly, "These are your *Halloween Ghost Challenge* ghost hunters!"

"Ghost hunters?" Natalie swiveled to look at Harper and Alice. "No one said anything about *hunting* when we signed up."

Natalie didn't love the sound of that term. Worse, she wasn't sure how the actual ghosts felt about it and was too afraid to glance at them to find out.

Alice waved her concern away. "It's just marketing. Right, Harp?"

Harper smirked at the nickname Alice had apparently bestowed upon her but nodded. "I have to agree."

Maybe they were right. The show certainly seemed designed to be all about grabbing the ratings, right down to the selection of the participants.

It was pretty obvious already how and why they'd been cast. The skeptic, there to debunk the paranormal, pitted against the believers. The producer would no doubt reinforce the stereotypes and conflict between them in editing.

Then there those who seemed strictly there to get on television. Whether to revive a dead career—that would be Tiffany who hadn't had a success since hitting puberty two decades ago. Or to further a career —like the YouTuber looking for more millions of followers and perhaps sponsorship deal dollars.

Madame Letisha fit into that category too. No

doubt she hoped to expand what Natalie doubted was actually worldwide fame in spite of good old Monty's introduction.

Well, she was going to be disappointed, because the only thing Natalie intended on hunting this week was Letisha.

Chapter Nineteen

"Ma—Madame Letisha?"

Letisha cocked up a sharply sculpted brow high and looked her number one fan, Megan, up and down as she approached tentatively. "Yes?"

"Can I—I mean do you, would you, like something to drink? Or eat? I can get it for you," the woman rushed to finish.

"I don't eat or drink while I'm communing with the dead," Madame Letisha proclaimed as if it were a universal truth and she the wise oracle dispensing it to the commoners.

Megan's eyes widened. "Are—are there dead here now?" She'd whispered the question as if the dead wouldn't hear it if she were quiet enough.

"The dead are everywhere, my dear," Letisha extolled.

Natalie let out a snort. What a crock of bull. It was a perfect non-answer from a practiced charlatan. And worse of all, it worked. The rest of the cast drew closer to Letisha.

"Madame Letisha. Could you do a reading of the room? Tell us who's here with us?" Sam asked, always producing and no doubt well aware Letisha's act would make good television.

"I usually like to meditate, center my mind and soul before communing, but since you asked." She touched two fingers to her forehead dramatically.

Jake the cameraman moved in closer to catch Letisha's act in all its overacted glory.

"I immediately felt an energy when I walked in. Buildings have their own personalities," she said mystically.

Natalie didn't know about the building having a personality. But there were certainly a lot of personalities inside it in the form of a century's worth of ghosts that pressed closer now. They surrounded the group, literally coming out of the gilded woodwork.

"I sense an older man. He worked here. He says his name is... Art. Oh, wait. I also hear someone whistling."

"That's all documented online," Natalie said, unable to keep her mouth closed any longer.

The doctor skeptic raised one hand and exclaimed, "Exactly!"

"You found that online?" Harper asked softly.

"GhostHub investigation video," Natalie answered low.

"Ha! Good job, Nat," Alice piped in, with her usual vigor and non-modulated volume.

The outbursts questioning her idol's authority elicited a gasp from Megan the super fan.

It also spurred a sharply lifted brow from Letisha. "It's okay. I've faced a lifetime of doubters, yet I'm still here, doing the hard work needed to help those on both sides of the veil."

"Oh, jeezus." Natalie rolled her eyes, then noticed the camera was now on her. Uh, oh. She was going to have to learn to keep her mouth shut.

"Madame Letisha, can you give us any specific details about any of the spirits you're communicating with?" Sam asked.

"Of course. I feel..." She closed her eyes and pressed those apparently magic medium fingers to her head one more time. "A man..."

"That's real specific." The doctor snorted.

"Fifty-fifty chance she's right, dude," the YouTuber commented with a laugh.

"Older, but handsome. Well dressed…"

"She's talking about me!" Bobby LaRue, costume designer, was suddenly next to Madame Letisha pressed close to the medium. "Yes, girl. Tell them about the fabulousness that is me."

"He's silent." Letisha, dropped the hand that had been pressed to her forehead, finally reopened her eyes and shook her head. "No. He doesn't want his story told. He won't communicate with me."

"Well, *that's* not me. She's not a bad actor actually, but she's a pretty crappy psychic."

"She's not a psychic. She's a fraud," Natalie grumbled low.

Bobby LaRue whipped his head around, his stare pinned to Natalie.

"She can hear us." He swooped closer. "This one. Right here. In the hideous boots. You, girl! You can hear me. Can you see me too?"

She tried not to move but with Bobby pressing his face right up in front of hers she couldn't help it. Natalie pulled back.

The half dozen or so ghosts in the room reacted. Their discussion rose from a whisper to a din.

It was so loud to her ears Natalie barely heard when Sam asked, "Natalie? You all right?"

Heart pounding, Natalie nodded. "Yeah. Sorry. Thought I saw a bug."

"Or was it an orb?" Megan asked, before looking to Letisha for approval.

"Answer me! If you can hear me, say something," Bobby insisted, startling her again.

He pressed his face close enough she could see the pores in his skin beneath the make-up he wore. Or had worn at the time of his death, she supposed, since they seemed to remain in what they had on at the time of their passing.

She couldn't think too much about the logistics with him so close, demanding attention.

"Not now," Natalie bit out between clenched teeth.

"Not now?" Bobby drew back with a laugh and glanced around at the other ghosts. "She said *not now*."

A woman, whose hair and clothing looked like she'd stepped right out of old Hollywood, sauntered closer. "Why not now? You have something better to do?"

Even her speech was quintessentially that nondescript Mid-Atlantic accent Hollywood favored during the early period of movie making following the silent era.

"Later," Natalie whispered as softly as she could.

"Hoo, hoo! Later, she says." The starlet turned dramatically to the others with a tinkling laugh then back to Bobby. "So, let me get this straight. This one can both hear and see us but is pretending she can't. And that one over there can't see or hear us at all, but is pretending she can?"

"That about covers it." Bobby nodded.

"These livings make me glad I'm dead," the starlet said with a flourish.

"Lying is wrong." The little girl was back again, this time glaring directly at Natalie rather than her boots.

Why were little kid ghosts so much creepier than adult ones? She didn't know why but they sure as hell were. A shiver ran down Natalie's spine as the child scowled at her.

"You're right. Lying is wrong, sweetie. Unless you have a very good reason to. Do you have a good reason?" Bobby pivoted to ask Natalie.

"Later," she repeated softly.

He cocked up one heavily plucked brow. "When?"

Natalie lifted a shoulder in a small shrug.

Luckily the livings' conversation had carried on

around her. It sounded as if Madame Letisha was explaining orbs to the cast.

Even Harper and Alice were listening, although it looked like that was mostly so they could make snarky comments to each other behind Letisha's back. But the good news was, the private, mainly one-sided conversation she was having with the ghosts went unnoticed.

"Okay, how about I decide?" Bobby suggested. "After the others go to bed tonight, you meet us by the stage. Yes?"

She nodded, mainly to get them to leave her alone. Definitely not because she was anxious for this meeting.

It was only day one and Natalie had already been exposed, at least by the spirits, and now she had a ghost appointment. It wasn't a very promising beginning.

Chapter Twenty

"AH, AND SO SHE APPEARS," BOBBY SAID WITH a good bit of attitude when Natalie walked down the center aisle between the rows of theater seats.

Since it was two-thirty in the morning, Natalie almost hadn't appeared. The only thing that had her keeping her appointment with the ghosts after what had turned into a lengthy first night of theater tours and Letisha's lectures was that she was sure Bobby would come get her out of bed if she didn't come.

At least she'd remembered to disengage her microphone from her clothes and leave it in her bed. That way it would pick up Alice snoring and passing gas while under the influence of a pot laced gummy induced slumber and Natalie would be able to speak freely to the spirits. Luckily Harper had drugged herself to sleep too, so Natalie was free to sneak out.

The stage was dark except for the ironically aptly named *ghost light*. Apparently every theater kept one light lit at all times. The cast had learned about the superstition—that if the stage ever went dark the theater would fail—during tonight's very long tour.

It, and the exit signs, provided just enough illumination Natalie could make her way down to the front row and flop back into a creaky seat. She was already exhausted. Her back and her feet both hurt from standing around listening to all the many ghost stories, personal encounters and history the Stanley Theater staff members giving them a tour had to offer.

All Natalie wanted to do was crawl into bed, even if it was a roll-away in the dressing room she was sharing with Harper and Agnes. But the ghost world waited for no living so here she was.

"Please allow me to introduce myself. *I* am Bobby LaRue," the ghost said dramatically as he bowed to Natalie from center stage.

She nodded. "Costume designer from, I'm guessing, the nineteen-seventies?"

His thin brows rose. "Hmm. Good guess. I died in eighty-one. And you are?"

"Natalie," she answered, thinking the less she

revealed about herself to these unfamiliar spirits the better.

"Natalie…" he prompted.

"Natalie Chase from Mudville, New York," she elaborated, feeling the temperature of the air in the theater drop as the ghost population thickened.

"And are you a medium by trade?" he asked.

"Nooo," she said, elongating the word as she shook her head. "Just a shop owner."

"Really? Yet you communicate with the spirit world."

"Not by choice," she said, opting for honesty.

That earned her another signature brow lift from Bobby. "And what is Natalie Chase, shop keeper from Mudville, doing here in Utica at the Stanley Theater?"

"They're filming a reality television show about ghosts. Or more accurately, about how livings react to being trapped together in a haunted building, day and night, for a week. I was chosen as one of the cast."

"Is *that* what's happening? I'd wondered since none of you seemed to be actual actors. Perhaps that Letisha person," the starlet commented as she sauntered smoothly, seductively, across the stage toward Bobby. "This *reality television* business is another reason I'm happy I'm dead. Honestly, what happened to good old-fashioned acting with actual scripts?"

"Preaching to the choir, sister." Bobby shook his head before saying, "Natalie, may I formally present Evie Hartwell. Star of the silver screen."

"I made the transition from silent films to talkies seamlessly at a time when many others did not. And just as my career was really taking off, wouldn't you know it, someone up and murdered me. Right here in this theater at my very own movie premiere."

That information knocked any sleepiness out of Natalie. "You were murdered? How?" She looked for any signs of injury on Evie's ghost but saw none.

"The doctor concluded poison, though the murderer was never identified or brought to justice."

"Wow. I'm sorry. That's horrible. Although I have to say, you look fabulous." It never hurt to flatter the spirits.

Besides, Natalie spoke the complete truth. Evie would be eternally young and beautiful as well as dressed to impress.

"Aren't you sweet. Thank you." Evie smoothed her dress and looked pleased.

"I always said, there are worse things than dying at your peak." Bobby brushed his nails across the wide lapel of his lavender suit jacket. "Now, back to the introductions. Clara. Stop hovering and come out here, girl."

The child stepped out from the wings and into the glow of the ghost light.

"This is Clara Delaney. Singer. Dancer. And the one most likely to cause havoc among the livings whenever she can. She began performing with her parents in a traveling Vaudeville act at five years old, if you can believe that. The show came through here the year after the theater opened."

And Clara, obviously, never left. How tragic.

Natalie itched to ask what happened when Bobby literally stage whispered, "Influenza."

"Nice to meet you, Clara. I'd love to see you sing and dance—"

But Clara was already gone, skipping off the stage after sticking her tongue out at Natalie and saying, "Nope!"

"All righty." Natalie laughed.

"Don't worry. You'll get used to her," Bobby said with the flip of one wrist. "Next—"

Before Bobby could finish his introduction, a well-dressed, classically handsome dark-haired man stepped forward and delivered a deep bow. "Vincent Carlisle, at your service."

"Vinny bit the dust that same fateful night as Evie."

"Two deaths in one night?" Natalie asked.

Bobby nodded. "Mm-hm. That must've been one hell of a night here at the Stanley."

"Although I'm certain no one wanted to murder *me*. Everyone loved me. I believe I accidentally stumbled upon the poison meant for Evie."

"That's what you get for nipping a glass from that expensive bottle of champagne in my dressing room," Evie called from the seat in the audience where she'd draped her lithe body. "And for your information, everyone loved me too. I can't fathom who in the world would want to kill me."

The comment prompted a dramatic eye roll from Vincent. "No? I can think of a few. And I left you a box of chocolates, darling. It was a fair exchange."

"A box of chocolates you'd half eaten!" Evie accused.

"It was one piece," Vincent defended.

Poison champagne. Natalie was fascinated and wished—not for the first time—that she had her cell phone so she could search for more information.

They were both movie stars. Both died in the same location on the same night in the prime of their lives and at the height of their careers. There must be something online about the mysterious deaths of Vincent Carlisle and Evie Hartwell.

Natalie tried to commit the names to memory for whenever she did get access to technology again. Ugh. It was going to be such a long week.

"I have a question. If that's okay?" Natalie asked.

Bobby spread his hands, palms up, before him. "I live to serve...so to speak."

"Is there a former employee named Art here?" Maybe it was selfish, but Natalie would love to debunk completely Madame Letisha's earlier *reading*.

"He was here, for a time right after his death. Used to be a projector operator. But alas, he moved on," Bobby explained.

"He was a sweetheart," Evie commented with a sigh. "Of all the spirits who could have moved on, he was the last one I would have wished gone. Now, Vinny, for instance..."

"Yeah, yeah. Love you too, Evie, babe." Vinny replied, his tone dripping with sarcasm as he stood with his hands in his pockets in a perfectly casual leading man pose.

"We don't get to choose our fates, my dears," Bobby said philosophically.

He clapped his hands together once and glanced around the periphery of the dim theater.

"There are a few more of us you'll see lurking around. Edgar Winslow is in death, as he was in life, always in the same seat in the back row for every performance. It is in fact, the seat in which he died. Heart attack. Rumor has it he was involved in some scandal during his lifetime. He's not much of a talker so the secret remains as such. Sadly. I do love a good scandal."

"Oh, we know," Evie commented.

Ignoring her, Bobby continued, "There's also Harold Ludlow. The typical eccentric playwright. You'll see him hanging around scribbling notes, eternally revising his last work. Harry's career never quite took off, but that didn't stop him, then or now, from dispensing unsolicited and generally scathing reviews and critiques of every show that played here. A few too many experimental drugs during the sixties took him."

Bobby peered beneath the hand he pressed above his brows.

"I see you down there, Horace. You don't want to come up? No? Okay. Anyway, there in the back of the theater is Horace Wainwright. He was hired as an usher when the theater first opened in nineteen-twenty-eight until tuberculosis took him in nineteen-thirty. I suppose it makes sense he's so quiet since that is an usher's job, no? To silently guide patrons to their seats."

Natalie twisted in her seat and spotted the usher who'd been outside when she'd parked the car. "Hello, Horace. I'm sorry I ignored you earlier when my friends and I arrived."

The usher tipped his head and touched two fingers to his uniform cap in what she interpreted as an acceptance of her apology.

"That brings me to one more question for you, Natalie the shop keeper from Mudville."

Twisting back in her seat to face the stage, Natalie ignored what seemed to be her new name according to Bobby and said, "Yes?"

"Why *are* you hiding your ability from everyone, including your friends?"

It was a valid question. She had her reasons. Had wrestled with those reasons for months now. But now that she was here, it was looking more and more like her secrecy might be coming to an end.

Chapter Twenty-One

GHOST HUNTING WAS, APPARENTLY, STRICTLY a nocturnal occupation. At least as far as the Paranormal Channel was concerned.

That meant it threw the cast and crew off any semblance of a normal schedule. It had them sleeping for much of the day and waking in the afternoon to the coffee and breakfast foods provided by the catering staff before a long night of filming and supposed ghostly encounters began.

The schedule was enough to have even Letisha turned upside down and cranky. She'd snapped at one of the crew tonight and even had some less than kind words for her super fan Megan.

Natalie quite enjoyed seeing her facade crack.

Maybe the real Letisha would slip out and expose her for who she really was, for all the world to see.

But the worst part of the grueling schedule, more than the vampire hours, was that Natalie knew for a fact, beyond a shadow of a doubt, that it was unnecessary.

As far as she'd seen, ghosts kept pretty much the same hours in death as they did in life. Meaning they were usually active during the day and would have been absent at night *if* the nocturnal nature of the production schedule hadn't been interesting enough to keep them hanging around after dark.

"This is boring." Alice yawned one more time as she stared at the lights on the electromagnetic field meter in Natalie's hand.

Indeed it was. Did the machine even work? Or was it all bullshit?

Natalie decided to find out.

She spotted Bobby over by the food table, sniffing at an abandoned cup of coffee like it was a line of cocaine.

"Let's see if we can liven things up," Natalie said.

"How?" Harper asked, looking as bored and tired as Alice.

"We're gonna find some ghosts." Natalie smiled and headed directly for Bobby.

Arm extended, she thrust the meter not just at the man, but actually through him as he straightened and spun to face her with a, "Hey!"

The machine went wild as the formerly lifeless lights on the meter sprang into action. She pulled it away and the lights subsided before she thrust it forward again and watched the lights react one more time.

"Well, look at that. The damn thing works," Natalie said, mostly to herself.

"Are you done poking me yet?" Bobby asked.

"So wait. Does that mean there's a ghost right there?" Harper asked.

"That's what it means," Natalie said. She saw the expression of horror on Harper's face and added, "Supposedly. If you believe the experts."

Bobby cocked up one brow accusingly.

Yes, she knew he thought she was ridiculous for hiding her ability, just like Gabe did. Just like Liam. That was just too bad. The decision was hers to make. Although thoughts of Liam, and Gabe and home, had her heart twisting.

She needed more of a distraction than standing around staring at the little black box in her hand.

"Shall we find some more?" she asked, turning to Harper and Alice.

"Uh, yeah. Sure." Harper nodded looking anything but sure.

"Can we look near the bathroom?" Alice asked. "That coffee I drank is starting to kick in."

Oh, jeez...

"Yes, Alice. We can." Natalie now knew more about Alice's toilet schedule than she ever wanted to.

They all did. And if the producer deemed it, and didn't edit out Alice's frequent bodily functions, so would the world once the show aired.

Just outside the dressing room and bathroom they shared, Natalie was lucky enough to find Evie.

Alice rushed her white Skechers Slip-Ons inside to use the bathroom. Meanwhile Natalie, fearing Evie was going to disappear if she came at her with the device, said, "For the audience at home, we're using a device to monitor spikes in the electromagnetic field which can be indicative of the presence of a spirit."

She raised a questioning brow then extended her arm with the EMF meter slowly.

Evie rolled her eyes, spread her arms dramatically and said, "Go ahead."

The machine's lights began to flash and bounce once again.

"There's a ghost here too?" Harper whispered.

"Sure looks that way... if the machine is working correctly."

"How come I don't feel anything? Shouldn't I feel something? Cold or, I don't know, a presence?"

Evie let out a huff and walked at them, then through them, sending a visible tremble through Harper.

"Oh my God. I felt something!" Harper grabbed Natalie's arm.

"Me too," Natalie agreed, glancing over her shoulder at Evie and mouthing silently, *"Thank you."*

"Of course, darling. Want me to round up a few of the others for your little show?"

Natalie nodded, then turned back to Harper before she got caught seemingly communicating with what to Harper looked like nothing but an empty hallway and a wall.

But when she turned back, she saw more than Harper looking a bit wobbly from getting up close and personal with Evie. More than Alice coming out of the dressing room wiping her damp hands on her sweat suit. She saw Jake the head cameraman, camera in tow, heading straight for her.

That was new. Camera number one had mostly stayed glued to Madame Letisha since she put on such a good show. But now, Jake was here. And focused on her, which, as usual, had her freezing.

God, how she hated cameras.

Harper sprung to action, thankfully. "Alice. A ghost just walked right through me. I swear."

"I miss all the good stuff," Alice grumbled.

"Maybe it's still here." Harper looked hopefully at Natalie.

Natalie shook her head. Evie had left but she couldn't say that, so she said, "Nope. See the lights? There's nothing." She held up the EMF meter as proof.

"Can we go try someplace else?" Harper asked, apparently recovered from her encounter and raring for action.

"Uh, sure. We'll give it a try."

Chapter Twenty-Two

Natalie led the procession. Or rather, Jake did, walking backwards ahead of them.

Besides the fact she feared he was going to fall down a flight of stairs or something doing that, and then die and she'd have one more ghost to deal with, she didn't love being the focus of his lens. Not at all.

She'd have to give him something else to focus on. And in the back of the theater, young usher Horace provided just the thing.

"There's a presence here. Look." She held the machine near Horace.

His eyes widened as he glanced at the device and then at her.

"It's okay," Natalie said, worried the already shy spirit would bolt and possibly be emotionally scarred for the rest of eternity. "It won't harm you. It just let's everyone who can't see you, know that you're here. That's kind of fun, right?"

Horace visibly swallowed—she was endlessly fascinated that the habits and ticks from life carried into the afterlife—then he nodded. She treated him to a smile that only he could see, then turned around to face the others.

The numbers of both living and dead had increased considerably. It seemed the members of the cast and crew who had been glued to Madame Letisha's side for tonight's investigation had jumped ship. Here they all were surrounding Natalie.

Derek the YouTube star, dressed as if he was about to hit the skatepark rather than hunt ghosts, stepped forward. "You talk to them like they're... human."

Natalie frowned. "They are human. The only distinction is living versus dead."

Amid a round of applause from the dead in the area, Evie nodded. "That's what I've always said."

"Exactly!" Vincent agreed.

Bobby LaRue, clapping loudest of all, said, "Preach, girlfriend."

She'd listened and learned when the Mudville spirits had lectured her on ghost etiquette. Apparently that paid off in helping her win the trust of the theater's inhabitants.

"And do they, like, communicate back to you?" asked Tiff the former child star, who'd proven herself to be generally clueless regarding anything ghost related.

How did she answer that question? This was getting tricky, which shouldn't be a surprise. Straddling the fence between lies and truth was bound to get uncomfortable.

It had seemed simpler in the planning stages. One, continue to deny her ability to her friends in an effort to preserve the status quo of the life she'd built in Mudville. The life she loved. All while, two, using her ability to expose Madame Letisha.

That meant she had to pretend to her friends that her ghost powers were all an act, just like she'd done when she'd held that fake séance for the real ghosts last Halloween. At the same time, she had to convince the PNC people her ghost powers were real.

"Um, yes. Sometimes," Natalie finally said, noncommittally. She held up the EMF device closer to Horace again so everyone could see the lights jump in response.

"But do they respond with actual words that we can hear?" the doctor demanded.

"Not everyone can hear spirits," Natalie answered. Again, it wasn't quite what he'd asked, but it seemed like a good answer.

"But can *you* hear them?" he asked.

Natalie should have known it wasn't going to be this easy. Doctor Oliver Finch was over-educated with a superiority complex as well as a die-hard skeptic.

Fine. Time to up her game. Just as Madame Letisha came around the corner with Megan in tow, most likely to see where her entourage had gone, Natalie said, "Yes. Yes, I can hear them."

Another cheer went up amid the ghosts who'd lectured her the night before about the importance of coming clean about what she could do.

Little did they know her plan hadn't changed. As far as Harper and Alice and the livings in Mudville were concerned, this was all a really elaborate and well-crafted act and she was as big a fraud as Letisha.

"Natalie?" One of the production assistants saying her name had Natalie turning.

"Yes?"

"Sam would like you to come with me."

Her pulse sped. "Um, why?"

"It's just for a one-on-one. You can hand the EMF over to one of the others."

A one-on-one? This couldn't be good.

The summons had the feeling of being called into the principal's office in middle school. Downright frightening.

Her body reacted just like it would have then. Her heart pounded. Her breathing was fast and shallow. Her hands trembled and suddenly, she really had to pee.

Then she remembered she wasn't in school anymore.

The worst Sam could do would be to kick her off the show. Then she'd get her cell phone back and be able to go home to Liam and her shop and her own comfortably familiar ghosts.

Yeah. That wouldn't be bad at all. Harper and Alice could do plenty to embarrass Letisha without her. It wouldn't take much. Letisha was pretty embarrassing all on her own.

Natalie nodded and said, "Sure. No problem."

She turned and thrust the device toward Harper, who drew back, eyes wide. "I don't want it."

"Oh, here. Give it to me," the doctor scoffed. "Honestly, as if there are any ghosts here anyway."

Their resident skeptic spun to leave and ran directly into Horace who appeared too surprised to move out of the way. The device blinked wildly one more time in response.

Doctor Finch paused and stared at the device in his hand. "I'm sure if we got an electrician in here he'd tell us that is because of the electrical wiring. It's probably reacting to the exit sign."

"No doubt." The YouTuber nodded. "I got electrocuted once. Hurt like a bitch, but that video got over a million views. Well worth it. I'd totally do it again."

With those words of wisdom still ringing in her ears, Natalie exited the theater and followed the production assistant down the grand staircase to the lobby floor.

Chapter Twenty-Three

"Sam's right over there." The PA pointed in the direction of a couple of chairs and a stationary camera set up against one wall, before she headed off in the other direction.

Natalie straightened her spine, lifted her chin high, pretended her leggings and oversized sweater were battle armor and headed for the producer.

"Hello," she said, taking a seat before being asked to. "You asked to see me?"

"Yes, I did. Would you mind answering a few questions?" Sam asked.

"Not at all. Shoot." She forced a smile.

"During tonight's investigation you told Doctor Finch the spirits communicate with you. With words. Can you tell us what they've said?"

How the hell— That had only happened seconds before the assistant appeared. Sam must be watching a live feed from Jake's camera.

Fine. She could handle this.

She had plenty of information she'd gleaned from those she'd spoken with. She'd tell it all to Sam, on camera. Everything she remembered. Then later, when their microphones were off so they could shower and change, she'd just tell Harper and Alice that she'd made it all up. Or researched the building before she'd come. Just to get one up on Letisha.

It was a good plan. Happy with it, Natalie nodded. "Of course. They said..."

"Could you repeat the question or give a little exposition for the viewers about what you're talking about before you answer?"

"Oh, yeah. Sure." God how she hated interviews and cameras. Drawing in a breath, she opened her mouth, then closed it again. Moving her gaze to Sam she said, "I'm *not* supposed to look at the camera, right?"

"No. You can. Please do. This is a confessional recording. All the cast members will make them. We want you to speak directly to the viewer at home."

"Oh. Okay."

Wishing they'd make up their mind and stop

changing the rules, Natalie considered how to word her response since now it seemed it was her job to introduce the question as well as give the answer.

"Since arriving here at the Stanley Theater, I've encountered a number of spirits who reside here. And I've learned some of their stories. It's been really fascinating. It seems there was not one but two murders here back in the early days after the theater was built."

"Murders?" Sam exclaimed.

"Yes." Natalie nodded. "Apparent poisonings. On the night of her movie premiere, film star Evie Hartwell died. She told me the doctor determined it was poison. And that same night right here at the same movie premiere, leading man Vincent Carlisle also died. Vincent believes he stumbled upon the poison meant for Evie. And Evie confirmed Vincent did take a bottle of champagne from her dressing room."

She'd been really getting into telling the story. Not only was it fascinating, but she would bet she had inside information the authorities at the time didn't have. Maybe, though it was almost a hundred years later, the mystery could be solved. Maybe they'd even exhume the bodies and test them both for poison.

Was that even possible this many years later? And how would Evie and Vincent feel about that? They might not like that idea. Gabe hadn't been thrilled about Liam cutting up his body in the cadaver lab.

Coming out of her own thoughts, Natalie glanced at Sam and got a look at the producer's expression. It wasn't good. It was the kind of look you gave a deranged person you were afraid of. Or at least afraid of setting off.

She'd better throw a few more facts out there. Things that would be documented and provable so she didn't look like a loon. "There's also a young girl named Clara here. She was a performer in a traveling vaudeville show with her parents. She died of the flu."

Sam's brows rose but she remained silent.

"There's an usher named Horace who worked here from the time the theater opened for business. He died of tuberculosis." When Sam's expression didn't change, Natalie continued. "There's a costume designer here named Bobby LaRue. He died in the early eighties."

"Of what?" Sam asked.

"You know what? He didn't tell me."

"You didn't ask?"

"No. I don't know. That seems kind of rude, you know? It's personal. I didn't feel right asking if he didn't offer up that information."

"Yes, of course." Sam's words didn't match her tone.

Worried she was coming off badly here, Natalie did what she always did. Dove in even further. "I do have one piece of information. Art, the projector operator who worked here for years and is said to haunt the projection room? He was here but he's since moved on."

"And you know this how?"

"Evie and Bobby confirmed it. He was apparently very nice and well liked among the other ghosts while he was here though."

Sam nodded with a noncommittal, "Mm-hm."

Natalie swallowed. "There's also an older gentleman who had a heart attack in his seat in the back row of the theater. He doesn't talk much, or at all that I've seen, but he's still here. He sits back there for every performance, even today. And then there's a screen writer. He is apparently quite the critic when it comes to reviewing the shows."

Natalie's enthusiasm waned with each revelation she made as Sam struggled and failed to maintain a passive expression.

Yup, those marching orders were going to come any second now.

"Anything else?" Sam asked when Natalie went quiet.

"No. That's it. So far."

"You think there's more?" Sam asked.

Natalie couldn't control the short laugh that escaped as memories of the ghost bat and Sybil and her horse flashed through her mind. "There's always more."

Chapter
Twenty-Four

"Shh. We have to be quiet. The mics are still on in the other room," Alice whispered inside the semi-private bathroom the three of them shared.

The bathrooms were the only places they'd been assured would be camera-free zones. And the microphones they'd all taken off so they could change into pajamas and finally get to bed—and hopefully to sleep before the sun rose—remained innocently *accidentally* forgotten on the vanity counter in the dressing room.

Natalie, toothbrush in hand, whispered back, "Why? What are we talking about?"

"How about what Sam wanted with you when you got pulled away?" Harper suggested.

"Oh, that. All the cast have to do this one-on-one confessional style video. I guess it was just my turn." She shrugged, pretending hers hadn't gone incredibly badly and any moment the door could open to reveal security guards there to escort her out of the building.

If they were going to stand around in the bathroom whispering, Natalie would have preferred some Letisha bashing. Or more plans to take Letisha down after the promising start they'd made tonight by stealing her camera time and entourage.

Even some gossip about the other contestants would have been preferable to talking about herself and her impending departure as she waited for the ax to fall, as she truly expected it would.

What Natalie didn't expect was Alice to whip out an iPhone from deep within her cleavage.

"Alice, I thought you turned in your phone," Harper mouthed, almost silently.

"No way." Alice wrinkled her nose. "That was my *old* one."

She waved one hand as if to dismiss the notion that she'd turn in her real cell phone. The one in her hand. The one that appeared to be the newly released iPhone.

"Now, shush." She pressed her fingers to her lips. "Watch and learn."

Silently compliant, Natalie and Harper watched as Alice deftly tapped the screen, then punched the side volume buttons before she turned the cell to face them.

On the screen was the Paranormal Channel app displaying the *Halloween Ghost Challenge* opening with no sound, but closed captioning turned on.

"Oh my God." Natalie gasped when she realized what she was seeing. It was the show and it was already out there for the world to see.

Her shocked words earned her a deep frown and a glare from Alice who pursed her lips together tightly and pressed one forefinger against them.

Harper gasped. "The first episode aired?"

Alice nodded. "Prime time. New episode every night until the Halloween live show."

"But we just got here," said Natalie, still trying to comprehend how it was possible.

The Paranormal Channel had culled through all the first night's footage. Hours of it. And had time to edit it into some semblance of a show to air tonight.

"That's how *Love Island* does it. What's filmed the night before makes up the episode the next night."

So Natalie was on a reality show that could be directly compared to *Love Island*? Ugh.

Meanwhile Montgomery had appeared on screen

and the closed captioning began to stream beneath his image.

Natalie leaned in closer.

"Eight people. Five nights. One haunted theater. Will they survive the *Halloween Ghost Challenge*?"

The shot switched to an image of the exterior of the Stanley while Montgomery narrated.

Built in 1928 the Stanley Theater in Utica, New York has its fair share of ghosts inhabitants. But for the next week, it will have eight more of the living variety.

The image switched to flashes of video taken of the cast. It looked like from their theater tour the first night. And of course, it included the three of them. This was possibly the part Natalie had dreaded the most. Seeing herself on screen. But with eight of them, no one person got a lot of airtime during the opening sequence. That was until they focused on each individual cast member.

Bold words appeared on screen over a still photo of the doctor while his name and profession appeared in smaller lettering beneath his picture.

THE SKEPTIC

Oliver Finch— Doctor

The words changed as the picture changed.

THE TRUE BELIEVERS

MADAME LETISHA— PROFESSIONAL MEDIUM

MEGAN FOSTER— SUPER FAN

A photo of Letisha filled the screen before it was joined by one of Megan. The two briefly shared the screen before the heading text changed one more time.

All the while Natalie anxiously waited, wondering and a little trepidatious about what title the producer had chosen for her.

THOSE SEARCHING FOR THE TRUTH

TIFFANY COLLINS— FORMER CHILD STAR

DEREK SIMMONS— YOUTUBER

Natalie let out a sniff as the photo of Tiffany, wearing a corset dress, was joined by one of Derek in his skateboard wear. That heading should have read *those searching for fame.*

But her annoyance didn't last long as she was faced with a photo of herself on the screen and then she read the title the producers had given her.

THOSE WHO CLAIM GHOSTLY ENCOUNTERS

NATALIE CHASE— SHOP OWNER

HARPER LOWRY— WRITER

ALICE MUDD— RETIRED TEACHER

"Claim? Like we're lying?" Natalie whispered.

"I look terrible in that shot. At least they got my name right," Harper mumbled.

"Shh!" Eyes wide, Alice pointed toward the other room where the microphones were as the video ran on.

Their resident B-lister, Montgomery Tristane listed only as HOST, was back on screen.

The closed captioning beneath read, "I'M YOUR HOST MONTGOMERY TRISTANE. JOIN US THIS WEEK FOR WHAT PROMISES BE THE SOCIAL EXPERIMENT OF THE DECADE ON HALLOWEEN GHOST CHALLENGE."

The show continued on.

According to the timer beneath the video on the app, it was going to be forty-four minutes long, not counting commercials. And there was no doubt in Natalie's mind that the three of them were going to stand there huddled around the cell gripped in Alice's gnarly fingers for every moment of it. And they did, until Alice's hand got tired from holding the phone and she leaned it against the tiled wall behind the sink.

So far, episode one looked to be taken up mainly by the welcome party and the tour the cast and crew took of the building.

Between editing, Letisha's dramatic nature and Tiffany acting overly frightened by every little thing, there were enough manufactured scares and cliffhangers before every commercial break to keep the show moderately interesting.

But audience boredom wasn't what worried Natalie. It was what episode two was going to entail. Because unlike the first night when the camera had mainly followed Letisha, tonight it had been all about Natalie—including that moment when she admitted she could talk to spirits.

And then there was one shot from tonight's episode that had her grabbing Alice's cell from where it was leaning on the sink against the wall and angling the phone so she could see it better.

"Is that inside the theater?" she asked when she saw an overhead camera angle of their tour.

"That's what I'm seeing," Alice said.

"There's a camera on the stage? I mean, besides Jake following us around," Natalie asked.

"It looks like it's maybe up in a catwalk above the stage," Harper said. "Why?"

"Uh, nothing. Just didn't realize we'd be seen from above, is all," Natalie said while her mind spun.

Her meeting with the ghosts...

Was that camera recording twenty-four/seven? And worse, was there audio as well as the visual evidence of what would look to millions of viewers like her sitting alone in the theater talking to herself while everyone else was asleep?

And that was before she'd spilled everything she knew about all the ghosts in the building in the confessional. With those two incidents together, she'd be lucky if they didn't ship her off immediately.

Chapter Twenty-Five

Sleeping in the windowless dressing room at the theater meant the only way to know day from night when Natalie opened her eyes was to check the time.

Unfortunately they'd taken her cell phone—which would have normally been the device she'd have reached for first upon waking. Just one more reason to feel its absence keenly.

She could have gone analog and referred to the sweeping hands on the big clock on the wall, placed there probably so performers knew how long until showtime, but the room was so dark she couldn't see the clock… or the wall.

Natalie might not know what time it was but she did know, based on the icy feel of any part of her body not currently beneath the blanket, that it was freaking freezing in there. Like break out the winter parka kind of cold.

This was a shocking change since Alice had just been complaining about the heat in the theater being turned on too high. And telling them how she kept the thermostat in her home turned down to fifty-two degrees at night. Cold air was better for sleeping, in her opinion. And she refused to fill up her oil tank more than twice per year, even though winters could drop to negative nine degrees Fahrenheit in Mudville.

The air was sure nippy now. Alice should be sleeping like the dead.

Natalie wouldn't be at all surprised if she'd be able to see her breath in the chilled air—if the lights had been on.

No matter what the hour, it felt like it was past time to get up. If only to make sure Alice wasn't actually dead. Frozen while deep in her pot gummy induced sleep.

"Psst. Anyone awake?" Natalie hissed.

"Nah-uh. Why is it so cold?" Harper groaned, her voice scratchy.

"I don't know. Maybe they ran out of heating oil? I feel like we need to get up and investigate."

"Go on. I'll stay here," Harper mumbled.

"All right." Natalie might as well get up.

She was wide awake now and she knew herself. Her mind wouldn't let her rest until she knew the answer to her question.

The glow of the emergency exit sign guided her to the doorway.

Yes, she was still wearing her owl-patterned flannel pajama bottoms. Yes, her sweatshirt did say *I Need Glasses* above a graphic of three various sized and shaped wine glasses. And the wording on the soles of her socks spelled out *Fuck Off, I'm Reading*. But this was not the time to worry about how she looked.

Something was wrong. She felt it in her bones— even if she couldn't currently feel her nose because it was so cold.

Natalie stumbled out of the door and into the second-floor hallway, thankfully lit.

The first person she found was actually not of the living variety, but that was fine. The ghosts probably knew as much if not more about what was happening than the livings.

"Bobby!"

"Natalie!" He imitated her with a smirk before dropping his gaze to take her in from head-to-toe. "Interesting outfit."

"It's what I slept in."

"You don't say?" he snarked.

"Why is it so cold?"

"Is it?" he asked.

Crap. Ghosts didn't feel cold, did they?

She let out a huff of breath and pointed to the cloud of vapor it formed in the cold air in front of her mouth. "See. It's cold."

"Yes, I see. I do know the producer is cussing a blue streak. And there are plumbers in the basement...along with a lot of water that I'm fairly certain doesn't belong there. And one unfortunately exposed butt crack. Now I truly understand why it's referred to as *plumber's crack*." Bobby gave a little shiver.

She blew out a breath, not for demonstration purposes this time, but out of frustration. "Sounds like a pipe burst."

"*And* she knows about plumbing. A *Jill*-of-all-Trades, so to speak." He smiled but Bobby's smiles contained as much attitude—and sarcasm—as the man himself.

"Oh, there you are." Evie came sweeping elegantly down the hallway. She too glanced up and down Natalie's outfit. With the swirl of one all-encompassing finger, Evie said, "You might want to change, dear. They're moving you to a hotel."

"Really?" Natalie's eyes widened.

A hotel. There would not only be heat, but phones and a television. And a real bed! This was the best-case scenario she could imagine.

"She looks excited," Bobby commented.

"She shouldn't be. It's the Hotel Utica."

Bobby's eyes flashed. "Oh my."

Like a record scratch, Natalie's glee came to a crashing halt.

Was the hotel not fancy enough for a starlet like Evie and an always critical designer like Bobby LaRue? As far as Natalie was concerned this hotel, no matter what it was like, had to be an improvement in comparison to the chorus dressing room she'd been occupying.

"*Oh my*, what? What's going on? What's wrong with Hotel Utica?" she asked.

Aiden Kim, the tech guy, came around the corner, interrupting the conversation before Natalie got her answer. He glanced around, as if looking for who she'd been talking to.

Playing dumb seemed like the best course of action. "Hey. Why's it so cold?"

"Pipe burst in the basement," he began.

She couldn't resist shooting Bobby an *I told you so* glance before focusing back on Aiden. "Oh no. What are we going to do?"

"Pack up your things. We're moving you to the hotel down the street. We'll still shoot tonight. You can wear a coat and gloves for that if you need to. But we can't have you all sleeping in a building with no heat. You'll be staying at the hotel until it's fixed. Can you go tell Harper and Alice? The van to the hotel is leaving in half an hour."

"Oh...Yeah, sure." Just when Natalie had every intention of remaining right there and finishing her conversation with Bobby and Evie, Aiden had other ideas. He remained as well. Standing right there. Obviously waiting for her to move first.

"I, uh, guess I'll go do that now," Natalie said.

"Yes, please," he said, still not moving.

"Okay. See you in a few... at the van," she added, hoping her dual message got through.

She needed the ghosts to know she wasn't done with this discussion but at the same time Aiden had to think she was complying with his request.

Aiden waited until she'd pushed cleared through the doorway to the dressing room. And by then she figured she'd better do as he'd asked. Get Harper and Alice moving so they didn't keep everyone waiting. Alice's post wake up bathroom routine alone could take thirty minutes.

She flipped on the lights and said, "Rise and shine. We're moving out."

But even as her roommates grumbled and she grabbed her bag to pack, she couldn't keep her mind from revisiting that nagging unanswered question.

What could possibly be going on inside Hotel Utica that inspired even the ghosts to comment about it?

Chapter Twenty-Six

As the van pulled up to the front of the impressive facade of the hotel, Sam stood and turned to face the group.

"Welcome to the Hotel Utica," she said, before referring to her cell phone. "According to the internet it was built in 1912. It's where the first beer was sold after the repeal of Prohibition. Judy Garland, Mae West, Mickey Mantle, Jackie Robinson, Amelia Earhart and FDR, just to name a few of many, all visited here."

"Well, finally. We're going to be treated to some decent accommodations," Alice said.

"It does look good," Harper agreed, shading her eyes against the afternoon sun as she peeked out the window at the building.

"And, in keeping with our show, Hotel Utica is reputed to be haunted," Sam continued.

"Of course, it is." Natalie sighed.

Reading off her cell, Sam said, "Calls come in to the front desk from unoccupied rooms, lights in the lobby turn off, guests see a housekeeper wandering the halls at two a.m., figures have been seen in the kitchen, and plates and salt shakers move on their own."

Sam lowered her cell and glanced up.

"This will be where you'll be eating and sleeping until we get the pipe repaired at the Stanley. But don't get too excited. Production will continue as scheduled. Dress appropriately for tonight's filming. It could get cold in there. You'll get your room assignments and keys when we're inside." She looked like she was done, but then she said, "Oh, and the televisions and phones have been removed from your rooms. The rule regarding contact with the outside world stands."

With that bit of bad news, Sam climbed out of the van.

"That's not a problem for us, is it?" Alice grinned.

Natalie widened her eyes and glanced around. "Alice. Shh."

"Don't worry. Nobody listens to us old ladies. I can do or say anything and no one cares," Alice said before gathering her purse to her chest. "Now, who has a dollar bill for me to tip the bellboy to carry my luggage?"

Natalie, Harper and Alice were—no surprise—assigned to share a room. Walking inside, Natalie saw there were two beds and an open-up sofa. So much for her dreams of a real mattress.

Being generous, she said, "I'll take the folding bed."

"Sounds good," Alice said with a bounce as she landed on one of the two beds and promptly withdrew her illicit cell phone from its place inside her bra.

"We can switch off and take turns if you'd like," Harper offered.

"It's all right. I don't mind." It wasn't as if Natalie was getting a whole lot of sleep anyway with all the worries and thoughts swirling through her mind. Her choice of bed wouldn't change that.

"What do you think about those ghost sightings Sam told us about?" Harper asked as she hoisted her suitcase onto the luggage rack.

Natalie lifted a shoulder. "I don't think there's a historic hotel in the world that doesn't have a few ghost stories attached to it."

Harper snorted. "I'm sure Letisha will have lots to say about them."

"No doubt." Natalie's laugh died on her lips when a dark shadow pressed close to her.

Unlike the usual ghost encounter, there was no face. No human form. Just an overwhelming feeling of dread. Like a weight compressing her organs, making it hard for her heart to beat. Impossible for her to draw breath.

She struggled to get air into her lungs and couldn't. Hand pressed to her chest, she opened her mouth but no sound came out.

"Are you okay?" Harper asked, concern furrowing her brow.

Natalie shook her head and stumbled for the door. She heard Harper say her name one more time but didn't wait. Didn't respond.

All she cared about was getting away from the entity, whatever it was. If that meant leaving the hotel, literally running outside into the street, then that's what she'd do.

She stumbled into the hallway and debated where to go. What to do.

Being trapped in the elevator with whatever that thing was seemed about as bad as being in a deserted emergency stairwell with it. Neither was ideal but they were on an upper floor and short of going out a ninth-floor window, there was no other way out.

Glancing up, she saw the black mass coming down the hallway after her. She'd have to make a run for it. Spinning away from the apparition, she crashed directly into Madame Letisha.

"Um, excuse you," Letisha said with a glare as she punched the button for the elevator.

Now was not the time for rivalries or sniping. Any other human being was an ally at this point.

Natalie glanced over her shoulder to see the shape moving closer. Turning back, she gripped Letisha's arms with both hands and gasped, "Get me out of here."

Letisha frowned until her gaze moved to the hallway behind Natalie. Then her eyes widened.

Could she see it too? If this thing was big enough, evil enough, that even a fake medium could see it, Natalie didn't want to stick around to learn more.

She was just about to flee for the stairs when the elevator door opened.

"Come on!" Letisha pulled her inside by one arm and punched the button to close the door.

Natalie stared at the gaping doorway, waiting for the doors to slide closed. Dreading the sight of the entity closing in on them before then.

Then, just as the dark shadow came towards the elevator, the doors slid shut.

When the car began its descent and the entity didn't come through the brass doors, Natalie collapsed against the back wall.

Finally able to breathe again, she looked at Letisha next to her. "You saw it too."

Letisha nodded.

"What the hell was that thing?" she asked. Letisha might be a faker when it came to being a medium, but she'd seen this thing too and that was good enough for Natalie.

"It felt...demonic," Letisha said, pale and looking as affected by the encounter as Natalie felt.

"Yes!" Natalie nodded. "Not like the other ghosts. They are just *there*. Like regular people, just dead. But this thing felt truly evil. Like I could actually physically feel its presence pressing against me."

The other woman watched Natalie with narrowed eyes as the door opened onto the lobby floor then, Letisha tipped her head. "Come on. I think we could both use a drink."

Natalie nodded and stumbled out after her former nemesis. The events of today definitely called for a truce.

Letisha raised one hand to the bartender and said, "Two bourbons, neat." Then she collapsed into one of the chairs.

Natalie flopped into the other chair, her legs still wobbly, and accepted the bourbon even though it wasn't her drink of choice.

"These go on the PNC account," Letisha said with such authority the bartender didn't question them, just nodded. Then she downed a good bit of the liquid in the glass held in her trembling hand.

Natalie did the same and felt the burn travel down her throat, causing her to cough, which earned her a raised brow from Letisha.

"Sorry. Went down wrong," Natalie said, then set the glass down on the table next to her chair.

"What's your deal anyway?" Letisha asked.

Recovering, or maybe just feeling brave from her shot of bourbon, she said, "I could ask you the same. What's *your* deal?"

After a pause, Letisha said, "I've felt ghosts since I was a child. It's like a presence. I can sense them. But I've never felt anything like that thing upstairs. And I usually can't see them either. It's a rare occurrence I see a full body apparition or even a shadow."

"Excuse me. I didn't mean to eavesdrop but did you ladies say you saw something upstairs?" the bartender said as he approached with a bowl of pretzels he set on the table between them.

"What do you know?" Natalie asked the man.

"Just that you're not the first. And it's not the only thing haunting this hotel."

Natalie shook her head. "We heard all about the ghost of a maid and flickering lights and mysterious phone calls and moving salt shakers, but this was nothing like that. This was—"

"Evil," Letisha supplied.

"Yes." Natalie nodded.

He shook his head. "Sorry. I only started working here this year. But I can ask around—Oh, excuse me. Customers."

When the bartender took his leave, Letisha's gaze pinned Natalie. "I told you my story. Your turn."

Letisha wasn't a complete fake. At least according to her own story. She just wasn't as skilled in communicating with the dead as she claimed.

Since they were bonding and all, this felt like a time for the truth.

Natalie drew in a breath. "I was electrocuted last year and technically dead for three and a half minutes. A doctor—my boyfriend actually though he wasn't back then—performed CPR and when I came back to life I could see ghosts."

"And talk to them?" Letisha asked.

"Yes."

"And they talk back to you?"

"Mm-hm. One of them back home in Mudville, Gabe, is my best friend actually."

Letisha's eyes narrowed. "You know what, Natalie? You don't have to like me. But you don't have to lie to me either."

With the shake of her head, Letisha stood and stormed off across the lobby, nearly taking out Alice along the way.

Chapter Twenty-Seven

"Yup. You're right. There's definitely something wrong with her. Look who she was sitting and having a drink with," Alice commented.

She and Harper stood staring at Natalie who remained seated. Shell shocked from both of her surprising encounters. First with the entity and then with Letisha.

Harper dropped down into a squat by Natalie's chair. "Are you okay? You looked like you couldn't breathe upstairs."

"I couldn't."

"What happened?" Harper asked.

"There's something in that room. On that floor."

Harper frowned. "Like what?"

Natalie shook her head.

How was she supposed to explain that thing or how it had made her feel? Harper hadn't seen it. Hadn't felt it.

It was hard for Natalie to believe, but Letisha had been easier to talk to about this. She'd seen it too.

That brought up a very good point. Harper had been in the same room with that thing and hadn't sensed it at all. But Letisha had seen it immediately. She and Natalie shared some similar sort of ability, at least on some basic level, that Harper and Alice did not possess.

"Do you think it's something you're allergic to? Like maybe mold in the carpet?" Harper asked as she continued to try and reason out what had happened, but she never would.

And that's why Natalie said, "I don't know. Maybe."

"We called Liam," Alice announced, plopping into Letisha's recently vacated chair and reaching for the woman's abandoned drink. She gave it a sniff then with a shrug, took a sip.

Natalie dragged her gaze away from Alice and back to Harper. "You called Liam? Why?"

"I mean he is a doctor and your boyfriend. The way you looked, I thought you might have asthma or something. That maybe you forgot your inhaler at home."

"Inhaler?" Natalie was still having trouble comprehending what had happened. What Harper was saying.

It was as if the entity had sucked away some of her brain. Some of her soul.

She shook her head. "No. I don't have an inhaler."

There was no medicine to help what ailed her. This ability to sense the supernatural had no cure.

It was like the thing had used that ability to target her. Her and Letisha. They'd both seen and felt that thing and it had come after them both.

Given that knowledge, Natalie was going to have to shift her whole outlook. About putting herself out there—possibly in harm's way—for this show.

And she was going to have to reevaluate her opinion of Letisha.

"You know what? I think we all could use something to eat. We've been sleeping days and up most of the night. Today we got yanked out of a dead sleep to move here. We need some sustenance. We'll all feel better after," Harper suggested.

Alice plunked down the now empty bourbon glass on the table and stood. "I feel better already. But yeah, I could eat."

"Do you feel well enough to stand?" Harper asked, gaze still glued to what Natalie suspected was her colorless face.

"I think so," Natalie said.

She proved it by pushing herself out of the chair and effectively ignoring the ghost in the top hat and tuxedo hanging out by the hotel's bar as they entered the restaurant.

"Remember, we can order whatever we want and charge it to PNC," Harper informed them. "There was a paper in our room from the production crew."

"Wonder if they've got lobster," Alice said as she followed along behind.

Natalie did feel much better after a bowl of French Onion Soup. The hotel's food was excellent even though they were eating off the dinner menu for what amounted to their breakfast. But she suspected she felt better not just from having eaten, but also from putting enough distance between her and the thing that had attacked her.

There was no way she was going back upstairs to that room *or* that floor. In fact, the elevator was suspect in her mind at this point. She wasn't thrilled about even being inside this hotel.

They were going to have to get her moved to a different room on another floor. She'd deal with that later—*after* she'd finished the cup of cinnamon tea and the slice of cheesecake she'd devoured half of already.

If she didn't think about the show, or the entity, or Letisha—if she only concentrated on the warmth of the tea and the cool sweetness of the cheesecake on her tongue—Natalie was for this brief moment in time and space, content. Calm. At peace.

And if she didn't look at the corner of the room where an elder man dressed in a hospital gown shuffled from one wall to the other before turning and doing it again, she could pretend her life was normal. That this was just a nice lunch out with two friends.

Until she heard a familiar voice raised loud enough in the lobby the sound reached her in the restaurant.

"I don't give a flying fuck what the Paranormal Channel told you. If you don't give me Natalie Chase's room number right now I will kick in every door of every room in this hotel."

Her eyes widened. "Is that Liam?"

Harper gasped. "We forgot to call him back and tell him you're all right."

If Natalie had been thinking correctly, she would have realized herself that she needed to call Liam and tell him everything was okay—even if she wasn't completely sure it was okay.

And now he was here.

She jumped up from her chair.

"Are you going to finish that?" Alice asked, pointing her fork at Natalie's dessert plate even though she was still working on her filet mignon.

"You can have it," Natalie said as she rushed toward the restaurant's exit.

"Natalie! Are you here?" That was Gabe's voice, yelling for her.

"Gabe?" Gabe was here too?

She cleared the doorway and sped into the lobby. She arrived in time to hear the front desk clerk telling Liam there was no answer in her room.

Then she saw Gabe standing in the middle of the room, hands cupped around his mouth. He was about to shout for her again while Millie stood nearby, but not touching him. If Millie did touch him, everyone in the immediate area was going to hear Gabe's disembodied voice shouting Natalie's name.

"I'm here!" she called out before Liam did something stupid like punch out the clerk and Gabe and Millie exposed themselves to all the livings in the lobby.

"Oh, thank God you're all right." Gabe rushed forward. Millie close behind.

Natalie didn't have time to properly greet Gabe or Millie as Liam turned and his gaze met hers.

He strode toward her, his long legs eating up the distance. When he reached her, his thick arms enveloped her, making her feel even better than the food had.

In Liam's embrace she felt safe. Protected. Even though she was still in this haunted hotel of horrors.

"Are you okay?" he asked against her hair.

"I am now," she managed while her face was still pressed against his chest. She pulled back to ask, "How are you here?"

"Harper called to say there was something wrong with you. Gabe and Millie and Ricky and Harriet were all with me when she called."

Natalie frowned. "Why were they all there?"

"We were streaming the first episode. But listen. Harriet used to be in the psychology field. When Harper told me which hotel you were in, Harriet completely freaked out. She said to get here immediately and get you out of this place."

She shook her head. "Why?"

Liam kept his hands on her, gripping her arms as he answered, "This building operated as a facility for the disabled for decades until it was shut down for neglect and mistreatment of the patients. Harriet feared it would be teeming with the ghosts of those who'd died here. And here you are in the middle of it."

Gabe nodded, grabbing Millie's hand so Liam was able to hear when Gabe said, "She was right, Nat. This place is a freaking hellscape of unhappy spirits. They're everywhere. You gotta get out of here."

Well *that* hadn't been in Sam's *Welcome to Hotel Utica* speech, but it sure did explain a lot. Such as Bobby and Evie's cryptic comments about the hotel. And the wandering spirit in the hospital gown in the dining room.

But it didn't quite explain that entity or the power it had over her.

Hand still grasping Millie's, Gabe continued, "Ricky and Harriet are doing a sweep of the hotel now, but I suggest we leave ASAP."

"Ricky and Harriet are here too?" Liam asked in the direction of Gabe's voice.

"Yes. Of course. Natalie needed us and they wanted to help," Gabe answered.

Liam frowned. "So I was basically driving what amounts to a clown car full of ghosts and didn't know it?"

Gabe rolled his eyes. "You'll get over it, big guy."

"Liam," Harper's voice from behind Natalie put

an end to the cross ghost-slash-living conversation. She rushed forward. "I'm so sorry I worried you."

"It's okay. I'm glad you called."

"Thanks for leaving me there alone to handle the bill," Alice said, doggy bag in one hand, her short legs motoring her over to where the group stood.

"It's all free, Alice," Harper pointed out.

"I know. And I left him a nice big tip on PNC's tab."

"Natalie Chase!" The sound of the PA's voice summoning her once again sent a tingle of dread down her spine.

She glanced up at Liam. "That's the production assistant. Sam must want to talk to me about something. I don't know what."

Liam let out a humph. "I might know. Is that microphone you're wearing live?"

Liam tipped his chin toward the mic that she had indeed forgotten was clipped to the neckline of her shirt.

Natalie swallowed hard. "Yes. They all are live."

Harper's, Alice's and even Letisha's.

Every single thing that had happened, that had been said, since they'd gotten dressed and boarded the van and arrived at the hotel had all been recorded.

She raised her gaze to meet Liam's. "I think it's time I tell them."

"You think?" Liam snorted.

"About damn time," Gabe said, still holding Millie's hand.

The sound of his voice had Harper's eyes flying wide. "Nat—"

"Yeah, Harper. I know." Natalie nodded. "That's the voice you heard. Can you guys follow me? All of you. I need to tell you all something."

The PA stepped closer, tablet in hand, headset on. "Natalie—"

"I know. Sam wants me. I'm coming." Natalie glanced around the group of both the living and the dead. "We all are."

The producer was about to get more than she bargained for.

Chapter Twenty-Eight

"Natalie... *and* Liam," Sam said, with a surprised lilt in her voice. "Pleasure to see you again. Does this mean you'll be staying for the remainder of the show?"

Liam let out a snort. "It means I'm taking Natalie and getting the f—"

"Babe. It's okay," Natalie interrupted.

She glanced around the mezzanine level where Sam had set up a confessional interview area similar to the one back at the theater. She wanted to make sure she was actually okay, as she'd promised Liam she was. To make sure there were no dark shadows creeping up on her.

The entity wasn't visible but the other spirits in the building were starting to gather. Much like back at the

Stanley, the camera set up on a tripod had attracted the attention of the curious dead.

About a dozen of the resident ghost population hovered nearby. Including one woman fully decked out in a ball gown. She was the oddity in this group. Most of the rest of them were in hospital gowns.

A ghost nurse circulated among the patients. None of them looked happy or displayed any indication of personality or individuality. Not like Bobby, or Evie or Vincent. It was almost as if they were all drugged. And maybe they all had been if tales of patient abuse were accurate. An overmedicated patient was a docile patient.

But none of them seemed aggressive or evil. Not like the dark entity she'd encountered upstairs. And for that she was grateful. As long as that thing stayed away, she'd be okay.

Probably.

"Really, I'm good. For now," Natalie said to Liam then turned to glance at Harper and Alice, and finally back to Sam. "You probably have a lot of questions. All of you. I'm ready to answer."

"Can we get three more chairs added to the confessional, please?" Sam said into her headset.

"Confessional?" Liam mouthed.

Natalie lifted one shoulder. "It's an interview kind of thing they do."

"Oh," he said, still gripping her shoulder as if he didn't trust she were safe. She didn't blame him. She wasn't quite sure herself.

She caught site of Gabe and Millie standing nearby. "Did you two want chairs?" she asked.

Her speaking to the air had Harper's brows rising while Alice frowned and turned in a circle as she looked for who Natalie had spoken too.

Gabe lifted Millie's hand in his and raised a brow in question.

"It's okay if they hear you," Natalie answered his unspoken inquiry.

"I think we're good standing. Thanks, Nat," Gabe said for all the livings to hear.

Harper's eyes widened as Alice drew back.

But it was Sam's expression that interested Natalie the most. As in, she didn't have any. Her face remained relaxed and passive.

How? Why?

Was it because Sam was a true believer—but even so hearing a ghost should elicit some reaction. Or, and this felt more likely, was Sam's lack of reaction because she assumed Natalie was lying and this was some party trick involving technology and assistants waiting just out of sight?

"What the hell was that?" Alice asked after hearing the sound of Gabe's voice.

"My friend, Gabe. He's a ghost," Natalie explained to Alice. She couldn't change what Sam did or didn't believe, but she could help her friends accept this new reality.

"He's the voice on the recording," Harper whispered.

"Yes, he is. But I have another confession to make. That wasn't recorded in your house the day of Letisha's visit. He wasn't there that day. No ghosts were. I'd cleared all the ghosts out of the vicinity so they wouldn't be harmed by the house cleansing. But Gabe and Millie made that recording for us later because you were going to hire Letisha again and I had to stop you."

Looking thunderstruck by all the information, Harper said, "Millie?"

"Gabe's girlfriend. She's here now. Millie, do you want to say hello?" Natalie asked.

"Hi—hello," Millie said shyly.

"Jeezus. You've actually been talking to ghosts. For how long?" Alice asked.

"Since I got electrocuted."

"All that time? And you didn't tell us?" Alice really was facing the existence of Gabe and Millie better than Natalie had expected she would. Better than Harper seemed to be, actually.

"Yes, Alice. And I'm sorry for hiding it. I didn't think you'd believe me."

"Hard not to believe you when we can hear them," Alice pointed out.

"That is a fairly new development. Gabe wasn't always able to be heard by other people until recently. Just by me."

"And they're like right here?" Alice asked reaching out one hand and swirling it through Gabe's abdomen.

"Right here," Gabe confirmed audibly, which caused a couple of raised eyebrows from Alice, but didn't inspire her to withdraw her hand right away.

Finally, she pulled her arm back to clutch her fingers with her other hand, saying, "Cold."

"What did we miss?" Ricky asked, skidding to a stop by the group, Harriet right behind him.

"Natalie's confessing everything," Gabe answered audibly, then realized his comment needed explanation for the livings other than Natalie. "Ricky and Harriet just arrived."

"Two more of my ghost friends from Mudville," Natalie elaborated.

"Yeah, they're all members of her 'ghost council'." Liam's explanation, which included air quotes, was delivered heavy on the attitude.

"Hey, you're invited to our meetings, buddy. Just because you choose not to come, don't blame us," Ricky said.

"Rick would like to remind you that you're always invited to our council meetings, Liam," Gabe repeated for Liam and the rest to hear.

"So not all of them can communicate?" Sam asked in her producer tone.

It made it sound as if she didn't believe a word Natalie said, but was willing to let her continue talking anyway because it would be good television.

"They can all communicate with me. I hear them, but other livings can only hear Gabe and Millie, and only if they're touching each other when they speak. We can only guess why that is. And trust me, I know how this sounds. Completely unbelievable. But it's all true. I really don't know how else to prove it. If Gabe didn't convince you..." Natalie spread her hands out wide with a shrug.

A production assistant set a chair behind Harper.

Just in time too. She looked about ready to pass out as she collapsed into the seat.

Alice perched on the edge of the chair they set behind her and said, "I believe you, Natalie."

"You do?" Natalie asked, her heart filled with love for the quirky old lady.

"Sure. My grams had the sight too. When I was little she was always talking to ghosts. Couldn't walk past the graveyard on Main Street without her saying hello to someone or another I couldn't see."

"Aw. Thanks for telling me that, Alice. I wish I'd known her."

The old woman lifted one shoulder. "Hell, go to the graveyard. Maybe her spirit is still there."

Natalie couldn't help but smile. "I will. When we get home. Maybe Ricky can help me ask around. He's like the mayor of the graveyard."

Ricky snorted out a laugh.

"*Mayor* in addition to the title of chairman of the ghost council? That might be too much for even Ricky to handle." Harriet chuckled behind him.

Sam, unaware there was a whole conversation going on she couldn't hear said, "You're wrong, Natalie. I do believe you."

"Do you?"

Sam nodded. "I do. And it's not just because I've

heard Gabe and Millie speak, although that is quite convincing. That first night, after we wrapped and everyone else went to bed, you went into the theater. Why?"

"I did, because at that point I wasn't sure I wanted to expose myself—what I could do—to anyone. Not my friends. And certainly not the whole television viewing world. But the Stanley ghosts figured out I could hear them and see them and they wouldn't let it rest. I can't blame them. I think it's pretty rare for them to be able to communicate so completely with a living. They demanded I meet with them, so I did."

"Were you aware of the camera above the stage at the time of that meeting? That we'd have both audio and visual of your meeting?" Sam asked.

"No, I was definitely not aware." Natalie shook her head. "I thought if Jake and his camera crew weren't around I was in the clear... as long as I remembered to take off my microphone."

"Speaking of your microphone," Sam began.

Natalie nodded, knowing where this was going. "You heard everything today. My conversation with Letisha. And when that... *thing* came after us."

"What *thing* came after you?" Liam's slowly spoken words were tinged with an underlying growl.

Natalie turned to glance at Liam and saw his jaw

was set, his eyes narrowed. "That thing is what freaked me out in the room. Why I couldn't breathe. Why Harper called you."

"Could you perhaps elaborate about this thing that made you not be able to breathe?" he asked, nostrils flaring as his chest rose with a breath.

"This thing, it wasn't a spirit. I could have handled the ghosts here at the hotel—although it would have been nice to know the sordid history of this building beforehand. This entity was something else. Something dark and powerful. Oppressive. And it only appeared to me and Letisha. It was inside our room with Harper and Alice..."

Harper grew impossibly paler at that, her knuckles white as she gripped the arms of the chair. Natalie forged ahead anyway. She had to get this out there in the open before that thing hurt someone.

Swallowing, she continued, "Neither Harper or Alice saw it or felt it. But out in the hall, when it was chasing me, Letisha saw it too. She called it demonic."

"That's it. We're out of here." Liam grabbed Natalie's hand and moved to stand when she pulled him back down.

"No. Wait. It's okay."

"It's not okay. When you use words like *demonic* to

describe things that are *chasing you*, it's time to get the hell out," Liam said, lips set in a firm tight line.

"I do think maybe it's confined to the ninth floor. It didn't follow us onto the elevator or downstairs. And I haven't seen it elsewhere."

Harriet nodded. "I did sense an incredibly oppressive darkness in the stairwell between the ninth and tenth floor. It is possible it's on those upper floors."

"True. Harriet and I didn't see it at all during our sweep, but we didn't search those upper unoccupied floors. They haven't been renovated at all. It looked abandoned up there so we left," Ricky said

That all didn't make Natalie feel any better, but she wasn't a quitter. No matter what Liam wanted. She was staying. "I don't want to leave, but there's no way I'm staying in that room. Or even going back up there to get my bag."

Harper let out a breath. "Well, neither am I. Whether I can see it or not, don't think *I'm* going back up to get our stuff. The staff is going to have to bring it down."

"We can arrange for your things to be moved to another room—" Sam began.

"On another floor," Natalie added.

"Not the fourth floor," Harriet chimed in.

"Oh, yeah. The fourth floor was bad," Ricky agreed.

"Not the fourth floor, please," Natalie added.

After a slight pause, Sam nodded. "Understood. You'll be reassigned sleeping quarters away from the ninth and the fourth floors. But is there any way I can convince you to go back into your original room with cameras and equipment and conduct an investigation?"

Natalie shook her head. "Nope. No way. I don't think even Letisha would say yes to *that*."

"I'd like to talk about Letisha and the prior interactions between the two of you," Sam began.

"Yeah, I need to apologize to her. And to you. I'd assumed she was a total fraud. Admittedly she does seem to exaggerate, for the sake of showmanship, I guess. But she's not without abilities. There is no doubt in my mind that she saw that evil thing, just like I did. I do believe she can sense spirits…"

"But?" Sam prompted.

Natalie drew in a breath. "I don't believe she can consistently see and hear them, communicate with them…"

"Or *befriend* them, the way you do?" Sam prompted.

Natalie nodded. "That's how it seems to me."

Sam planted both hands on the arms of her chair. "Well, thank you. This has been most enlightening."

Natalie raised her gaze to the woman as she stood. "I'm going to end up being an internet meme over this. A joke. Aren't I?"

Sam cocked her head to one side. "Possibly. But you know what they say. All publicity is good publicity. You might want to contact whoever is watching your shop for you while you're gone. I have a feeling they're going to have to bring in more help after tonight's episode airs."

Chapter Twenty-Nine

"You lied to me. And to Stone," Harper said after Sam had flipped off the camera and left.

"Harper, I'm sorry…"

"I heard them in my house. Stone heard them in the garden. But you never admitted it." Harper's tone sounded hurt.

"I didn't mean to lie. I just didn't want to confess the whole truth."

"Splitting hairs," Ricky said on a cough.

"You let Stone and me think we were crazy," Harper continued.

"I know. I didn't mean to."

"But why didn't you tell us? We're friends."

"I didn't want you to think I was crazy. Or a liar. I didn't think anyone would believe the truth, so I lied."

Pivoting, Harper turned to Liam. "You knew."

"I did." He nodded. "But it wasn't my secret to tell."

"But you believed her. So why wouldn't we? Her friends." Harper asked.

Liam laughed. "In Natalie's defense, I only believed her after there was so much evidence I could no longer deny the truth."

"You let me hire Letisha," Harper said to Natalie.

"I did try to talk you out of that. And not just because I thought she was a fake, but more because I was afraid she might be real. If anything had happened to any of the ghosts..." Natalie shook her head, remembering the horror of that night when she thought Letisha's cleansing might have worked and the ghosts were gone for good.

Gabe pursed his lips. "Aw. We love you too, Nat." When Liam scowled over the words, Gabe added, "As a friend. Of course. Don't worry, big guy. She's all yours. Promise."

The comic relief would have been appreciated if Natalie wasn't convinced she might have just lost one of her best friends. "Harper. I am so, so sorry. Tell me what to do to make it up to you and I'll do it. Anything."

Harper lifted her gaze. "Anything?"

"Anything," Natalie repeated.

"Can I write your story? If I change your name, of course."

She knew Harper well enough she should have expected this. She'd walked right into this one. But a promise was a promise.

Natalie drew in a breath. "Okay."

"And can I interview Gabe and Millie? And can they fact check my book?" Harper asked. Gone was the hurt, replaced by creative excitement.

"That's up to them." Natalie turned to face the couple.

Gabe glanced at Millie, then said, "Sure. We'd be happy to help."

"Hey, I want in on this too," Ricky said.

"I'm sure she'll take all the help she can get," Natalie assured. Then mouthed to Gabe, "Thank you."

He nodded.

"So are we done here?" Liam asked Natalie. "We can go home now?"

"You can't leave. The show's not finished until Halloween night," Alice said. "If Natalie leaves, Madame Letisha will win."

"Alice, there's no winner or loser. This isn't a competition," Harper pointed out.

"And we're not trying to take down Letisha anymore, remember?" Natalie reminded. "She helped me get away from that thing when I froze."

"Well, maybe we want to take her down just a peg. I mean she did charge me a fortune to walk around my house with some sage and chant nonsense," Harper said.

"I don't know what this show is besides a ratings grab but I do know Natalie doesn't have to be here for it." Liam scowled.

She covered his hand with hers. "I kind of want to finish what I started. Besides, I like the theater ghosts. They're fun. And oh my God, I forgot to tell you this. There's a murder mystery. Two of them were poisoned. Maybe you and I can try to figure it out, now that you're here. All of us together. Wouldn't that be fun?" Natalie glanced around.

"Solve a couple of murders for some ghosts. Sure. Why not. Not like I have anything better to do. I'm in," Alice said.

Harriet, Rick, Gabe and Millie agreed they were up for an adventure, as long as Liam got them back home directly after the show Halloween night, since they were pushing the boundaries of their geographical territory.

"Natalie!"

Natalie spun as Bobby, Evie and Vincent flew across the lobby. "Hi. What are you all doing here?"

"Who's she talking to now?" Alice asked.

"I'm assuming some new ghosts have arrived. You'll get used to it, eventually." Liam scowled.

Gabe snorted. "You never got used to it. You still get annoyed."

Liam bobbed his head. "It is annoying."

"You were attacked? The crew is all talking about it over at the theater," Bobby explained.

"I knew this place was bad news. I'm not even sure why we're here now." Evie glanced around.

"Natalie, darling, it must have been horrible. Are you all right?" Vincent asked.

Natalie nodded. "I'm fine. My posse from Mudville came to rescue me." She tipped her head at those behind her.

"Yes, so I see. I do love when we have fresh blood around, so to speak." Bobby looked the group up and down thoroughly.

"Bobby, Vinny, darlings, do you know what I'm thinking?" Evie asked, then without waiting for them to answer she said, "We have a fresh audience for our show."

"Show?" Natalie repeated.

"A number of us are, as you know, performers.

We've been putting on shows for each other and for the local spirits for almost a century. But now, we could perform our show for all of you!" Vincent exclaimed.

"I love it! We have to start planning right away. We'll do it Halloween day, twelve noon. You will stay, won't you?" Bobby asked.

Natalie nodded. "I have to stay for the live show Halloween night anyway, so yes. We'll stay." She remembered the decision wasn't hers alone. "Liam, you'll stay, right?"

"If you're staying, I'm staying. There's no way in hell I'm leaving you ever again."

Bobby pressed his hand to his heart. "Swoon! Oh my God. Where can I get one of him because I want one."

Natalie smiled. "That settles it. We all stay. Ghost performance Halloween day in the theater at noon. Followed by dinner and then the live taping of the show's finale at eight. Sound good?"

She turned to the livings, realized they didn't know what she was talking about and wouldn't be able to see the ghost show anyway, so she diverted her gaze to the ghosts.

"Good?" she asked again.

"Yeah, Natalie. Sounds good," Gabe said

indulgently. Then leaned in. "And when we get home we're going to talk about how quickly you replaced me with your new BFF Bobby over there."

She smirked. "You're still my number one."

"At least Liam won't worry about that one being in your life." Gabe tipped his head toward Bobby.

"No," Natalie agreed.

But as Bobby looked Liam up and down like Liam was a steak and Bobby was a starving man she decided perhaps she was the one who should worry.

Chapter Thirty

"It was nice of Sam to get us our own room. I don't think you're ready to share a room with Alice," Natalie joked, although she wasn't really in the jovial mood. "And I'm not sure Harper wanted to share a room with me anymore."

The look of hurt on Harper's face was going to stay with her for a while.

Liam leaned out of the bathroom doorway, toothbrush in hand. "Sam owes you at least a room of your own. You're going to make this show for her. She knows ratings gold when she sees it."

He disappeared back into the bathroom and she heard the water running in the sink.

They had a gorgeous room with a king-sized bed

and a bathroom almost as big as her apartment back at the train station.

It was a really nice hotel...even though it was super haunted. And might have a demonic infestation.

The sound of the water cut off and Liam appeared again, in all of his shirtless glory.

God how she loved when he walked around shirtless...and pant-less.

Liam in only underwear was perfection—even when he was lecturing her. Like now.

"And Harper is fine," Liam continued. "She was going back to her room to start plotting her new book about you so I wouldn't worry about it."

He crawled onto the bed and plucked his cell phone from her hand, tossing it onto the side table.

"Hey! I haven't seen my phone for days." She wanted to look at the store's social media and see what trouble Jules was getting her into by posting unsupervised. Then there was the store email she needed to check.

"And I haven't seen *you* for days," Liam said, his voice low and sultry as he moved in on her.

He pulled her down lower on the bed and straddled her legs. Running his hands up her leggings and beneath the hem of her T-shirt, he looked like a man on the prowl.

She knew where this was going. "I have to be back at the theater for tonight's filming in an hour."

He bobbed his head to one side. "Good chance you're going to be late."

Judging by the hard length straining the fabric of his underwear, she could see why he'd said that.

"I have to meet the rest of the cast at the van outside the front doors," she said as he slowly tugged her leggings down.

"I'll drive you to the theater. *After*," he said.

She didn't have to ask *after what* as he tossed her leggings to the floor.

"God, how I love when you're commando," he groaned.

"I was in a bit of a rush to get dressed today," she said by way of explanation for her lack of underwear.

It was too cold in the theater to take time to locate a clean pair of underwear amid the mess of things piled in her bag. With a nice warm van waiting for them on the curb to take them to the hotel, Sam is lucky she didn't come outside in her pajamas and a jacket.

"Don't care why. Just like it," he said as he spread her legs wide and leaned low between her thighs. Then he paused, his gaze meeting hers. "We are alone, correct?"

She knew what he was asking and answered, "There are no ghosts in our room." Amazingly.

Not the Mudville ghosts, who were planning on hanging out in the restaurant bar where they could people-watch and enjoy the aroma of the food they couldn't eat. Not the Stanley spirits, who'd rushed back to the theater to work on their show. And not the hotel ghosts, who were she didn't know where but who thankfully were not here. That was all she cared about.

"Good," Liam said and lowered his head again.

Her eyes drifted closed at the first feel of the heat of his tongue on her core.

If there were awards for foreplay, Liam would take the gold medal. Or the blue ribbon. Or whatever.

The man had her gasping for breath in mere moments. Her hands were in his hair and her hips off the bed minutes later. Then she was coming so hard she wouldn't have known or cared if there were ghosts in the room.

Liam sat up, a wry smile on his lips. "Still worried about making that van?" he asked.

"Just come here, you," she said, pulling him down on top of her.

As he slid inside her, she knew, she was definitely

going to be late. And she couldn't give a crap what Sam said about it.

Chapter Thirty-One

Natalie had been waiting for the knock on her hotel room door. Although she'd expected—and dreaded—that it would come much earlier than this.

Luckily it hadn't come twenty or so minutes ago. Then she and Liam had been nearing the culmination of a most enjoyable, not to mention energetic, romp in that big king-sized bed with too many pillows—most of which were now on the floor.

That timing would have been extremely inconvenient for all of them—Natalie, Liam and whoever was currently pounding on her door.

As it was, Liam was satisfied and smiley even in the face of this very loud interruption to their post-sex bliss.

Luckily, she'd had time for a very quick shower and they were both dressed. They'd been about to leave to get Natalie to the theater if not quite on time at least not horribly late when the knock came.

She pulled the door open and saw exactly who she expected—one of the PNC crew. Sam's production assistant Paulina to be exact. Though she was looking more panicked than Natalie's tardiness warranted.

"Oh my God. Thank goodness you're here," Paulina gasped, bracing against the doorframe as she struggled for breath.

What was this panic about? Of course Natalie was there. Did Paulina think that Natalie had gone missing? That she'd run away, absconding with a bag full of free filet mignon she'd charged to the PNC account in the restaurant?

"I know I'm supposed to be at the theater—" She began to explain but Paulina waved her off.

"No. I need you here."

"What do you mean? Why here? What's happening?" she asked.

"Sam left Letisha here at the hotel with a camera and a sound guy to investigate the upper floors, while she went to the Stanley with the rest of the cast and crew."

Natalie drew back. "What? And Letisha agreed to go back up there to investigate that evil thing?"

Paulina nodded. "Yes. And it started out fine, like any other investigation. For like the first ten minutes. But now there's something wrong."

"*What's* wrong?" Natalie demanded.

"The stairwell door slammed shut and no one can get it open. They're locked up there on the tenth floor. The crews' walkie talkies aren't working. We stopped getting the live feed from the camera. Natalie, I'm worried."

"You should be! Of all the stupid ideas..." She could only imagine the nightmare of what could be happening up there.

And though she had no love lost for Letisha, even after their recent demonic bonding experience, she couldn't leave her up there, in trouble. Not when she could do something about it.

What could she do? Natalie wasn't really sure. She'd have to figure that out on the way.

"Take me up there," she demanded.

Liam had come out of the bathroom to hear the last part of the conversation and said, "Whoa. No way are you going up there."

"I have to. I can't leave them up there with that thing."

Jaw clenched, he drew in a breath. "Then I'm going with you."

"Damn right you are. I'm not completely insane enough to go up there alone."

At that thought she realized she *wasn't* here alone. She had more help on her side than just Liam.

The ghosts.

She needed to find them. Both the Mudville ghosts and the theater ones. She'd need all their help if she had any hope of fighting that thing.

And while they were at it, an exorcist might not hurt.

"I need you to call someone at the theater."

"I already called Sam. The minute it happened," Paulina said.

"It's not Sam's help I need. I need someone on site at the Stanley to tell the theater ghosts I need them here with me. It's urgent."

"But none of the cast or crew can talk to ghosts except for you and Letisha."

"That's technically not true. The cast and crew might not be able to hear the ghosts, but the ghosts can hear them. If you tell them I need them here, the spirits will understand."

And they'd come to help her. She knew they would.

She strode out into the hall and grabbed the house phone located on a table between two chairs.

Dialing zero for the front desk, she said when they answered, "Do you have a paging system for the lobby and the restaurant area?"

"A paging system? No, ma'am. This isn't Walmart."

Attitude much?

She squeezed her eyes closed and regrouped. "Yes. Of course not. I'm sorry. Can you possibly transfer me to the hotel bar?"

"One moment," the snide desk clerk said before she heard a click.

A couple of rings later, a male voice said, "Joseph speaking, how may I help you?"

"Yeah. Hi. I'm looking for some friends of mine who said they were going to the bar tonight."

"What do they look like? I'll see if I can spot them."

"Um, yeah, they're hard to describe. Could you maybe just yell?" she asked.

"*Yell?*" he repeated, as if it were a dirty word. Unfathomable that she'd ask him to do such a thing.

Was she going to have to take the time to go all the way downstairs to try to find Gabe and the gang when Letisha needed her upstairs? Just because the employees of this fancy hotel refused to raise their voices to help locate a patron?

"Please, I know this is out of the ordinary, but if you could just announce in a moderately loud voice that there is a call for Gabe and Millie from Natalie. And that I need them to meet me on the ninth floor."

"All right. I'll give it a try," he agreed.

She breathed out in relief. "Thank you."

Natalie heard the bartender repeat the message perfectly. Then heard nothing but bar noise and chatter.

She replaced the receiver and said, "Let's go."

No need to wait. The ghosts would understand.

If they were within hearing distance of the bartender, at least one of them would figure out she needed help. Harriet and Ricky had felt the darkness on the ninth floor and Gabe and Millie had heard Natalie say she'd never go back up there again. They'd know her summoning them upstairs meant there was trouble.

But that was only *if* they were still here. How she prayed they would be. She could only hope they hadn't decided to go for a stroll to take in downtown Utica.

"What are you planning to do? Do you even know what to do?" Liam asked as he kept pace with her as they strode down the hallway behind Paulina.

"Not really. Actually, could you search that for me on your phone?" she asked.

He frowned. "Search *what* exactly?"

"Try *how to fight demonic apparitions.*"

"Are you serious?"

She shot him a glare. "Do you have a better idea right now?"

"Fine. I'll search," he scowled and pulled out his cell.

A room service tray sat on the floor outside a door in the hallway. Natalie bent and scooped up the salt shaker as they strode past.

Salt was good. Right? Witches liked salt. The good ones. It was good for protection or something like that. She could use all the protection she could get.

She probably should have taken the knife too, but it was only a butter knife, not a steak knife. And she didn't think stabbing the entity would do any good anyway.

"You find anything?" she asked Liam as they walked. Damn, this hotel was big.

"Believe it or not, there's a YouTube video." He handed the cell over to her.

The first video was useless. It was all about embracing truth and denying lies to fight the demons in your life. Since she wasn't about to enter into a debate with this thing and she wasn't even sure it had a brain or a mouth or ears, she navigated to the next video.

It was titled *How to Overcome Demonic Attacks*.

That sounded promising. She opened it and realized it was just a preacher preaching.

"Ugh. This is no help." She thrust the cell back at him.

Where was a person supposed to go to learn what she needed to know?

She'd just have to figure it out on her own.

Paulina came to a stop at the elevator and Natalie eyed the legs of the table there, wondering what kind of metal they were made of.

Silver was for werewolves. Wooden stakes for vampires. But wasn't lead good for something too? And what would work on demons? Ugh. She was not prepared for this.

She gripped her salt shaker harder as Paulina punched the *up* button three more times.

Liam handed the cell back to her saying, "Here."

"What is this?"

"It's an article about getting rid of ghosts in your house. It's on a real estate website, of all places, but it was the closest thing I could find to what we need. The church really has the search results for *demons* all sewn up. But since they keep referring to addictions and porn and anger, I don't think the kind of demons they're talking about fighting are the same as ours."

"I think you're right." But she probably should have checked the hotel drawer for a bible anyway. She was going to need every weapon in the demon hunter's arsenal for this.

Glancing down at the article, she saw that first on the list was sage. Dammit, that was what Letisha used. She hated that Letisha was right.

Second on the list was talking to the entity. Yeah, that wasn't going to happen.

But third on the list was, *hallelujah*, salt.

Chapter Thirty-Two

"Natalie!" Gabe, Millie's hand held in his, called her name the moment the elevator doors opened on the ninth floor and Natalie stepped out.

She, Liam and Paulina—looking less than comfortable to be up close and personal with a ghost she could hear but couldn't see—turned toward the sound of his voice.

"You're here." Natalie rushed toward the group of the four Mudville ghosts down at the end of the hallway.

"We got your message. What's happening?" Ricky asked.

"And why are we back up here on this floor?" Harriet asked with a visible shudder.

"We think that evil dark thing has Letisha and the

crew trapped upstairs. The stairwell door won't open. And none of the communications are working."

Ricky blew out a breath. "Whoa. That's nuts."

Harriet shook her head. "This thing is powerful if it can block the door as well as the technology."

That wasn't what Natalie wanted to hear, although she'd had the same thought herself.

"Natalie! Have no fear. Alas, we are here to help!" The sound of Bobby LaRue making a dramatic entrance had Natalie spinning.

She saw a group of the theater ghosts heading her direction.

"We heard what was happening on that producer woman's radio," Evie explained.

"So we stopped by the Catholic Church on the way here and grabbed a priest." Vinny thrust forward the confused looking ghost of an older man she didn't recognize. And he was indeed wearing a priest's collar and clutching a Bible to his chest.

"What's happening?" Liam asked, the familiar sound of frustration in his tone.

"Sorry. The Mudville ghosts are all here and the Stanley ghosts just arrived. And they've brought along... a ghost priest."

Paulina's eyes widened. Natalie couldn't blame her for the reaction. She'd never have imagined those words ever coming out of her own mouth. But right now, a ghost priest might be exactly what they needed.

As they made their way toward the emergency stairs at the end of the hall, Natalie caught the new arrivals up on what they'd missed. She filled the priest in on everything she knew about the entity, with Harriet's help.

Paulina provided logistics information about the PNC team's location. Then there was nothing left to do except face the shadow behind the steel door they all currently stood in front of.

Natalie drew in a breath, reached out her hand and turned the knob. Eyes wide, she spun to Paulina. "It turned."

Paulina shook her head. "It's not *that* door that's stuck shut. It's the door at the top of the stairs that leads to the tenth floor where Letisha went to investigate."

"But it makes sense that door might be locked. Those upper floors are not renovated. The hotel wouldn't want any guests wandering up there," Natalie pointed out.

"Perhaps, but it opened just fine when the team went upstairs."

"Oh." She should have known it wouldn't be that easy. Not that simply getting the door open was their greatest challenge. Facing the entity was the biggest problem.

The darkness of that thing was palpable. It was already making her feel nauseated. If it felt this bad down here, on the floor below, she didn't want to imagine how bad the evil would feel one flight up. But she supposed she was going to find out.

"Okay. So let's go up and try the next door." Heart pounding, Natalie swung the door open wide and stepped through.

At her first step into the stairwell she immediately felt the emotions bombard her.

If hate and anger could be felt, viscerally, externally, this is what they'd feel like. It had her standing in front of the door marked 10TH FLOOR, not moving. Not wanting to.

Liam moved up next to her and reached out to try the doorknob only to drop his hand again when it didn't turn. "She's right. It feels like it's locked."

"Emergency stairs and fire exit doors in public buildings can be locked from the one side, but not from the egress side. So even if it is locked to our side, it can't be from their side. So if the team up there were capable of reaching the door, they would be able to open it to get out," Ricky supplied. When the ghosts, plus Natalie, turned to look at him, he shrugged. "I was a volunteer fireman for thirty years."

"So that means that *thing* is keeping the team from opening the door and leaving. Not a lock." And that was not comforting. Natalie turned to Liam. "Can you kick it in?"

His dark brows rose. "No."

"Isn't that what you military men do? Kick in doors." They did it all the time on television.

"Yes, Natalie. That is sometimes what we do, but the hinges are on the wrong side. The door opens towards us. And it's a three-inch thick metal door. I could kick that all day and it's not going anywhere."

"Can you take it off the hinges? Blow it off or something?" she asked.

Those brows rose impossibly higher. "Sure, Natalie. Oh wait. Silly me forgot to bring my C4 and breaching charges with me to Utica to see my girlfriend."

She pressed her lips tight and narrowed her eyes at him. "No need to get snippy. We're kind of desperate here."

"I think you two are forgetting one thing," Gabe began, holding Millie's hand so Liam and Paulina would hear. "None of *us* need you to open that door."

Her chest clenched at the thought of the ghosts going in there on their own and fighting that thing, even though she was in no way excited to go in there with them.

"Exactly. Come on. Let's get that thing!" Ricky looked around the group of spirits. "Who's with me?"

"I'll go." Vinny, playing the role of hero, raised his hand.

"I'm coming too. I worked as a counselor for most of my adult life. I might be able to talk to it," Harriet offered.

"I'm coming, of course," Gabe said, then turned to Millie. "I think you should stay here with the women."

Evie rolled her eyes. "I see times haven't changed."

"For good reason. I think I should stay here with the women too. To protect them," Bobby LaRue suggested.

The priest, who Natalie hadn't been sure could talk because until now he had remained silent, took a step forward. "I'll go in first."

"You sure, Father?" Ricky asked.

The old man, who looked slight in stature but large in confidence, nodded. "I've spent a lifetime fighting evil."

"Are you certain you're all going to be all right?

What if this thing attaches to you? Or just like eviscerates you?" Natalie asked.

A blood curdling scream cut through the air, muffled but audible in spite of the heavy metal door.

"Letisha," Paulina breathed.

"There's no more time. We have to go now." The priest turned and walked through the door.

Vinny, Rick, Harriet and Gabe followed, but only after Gabe delivered one last backward glance first at Millie, then at Natalie.

"Be careful!" Natalie called after him, but he was already through the door and out of sight.

She pressed her palms against the door and felt icy cold radiating from the metal. "Being on this side of the door while they're all in there is horrible."

"Not as horrible as being on the other side, I imagine," Bobby commented.

Liam pulled Natalie back against his chest, wrapping his arms around her. "I'm glad you're on this side."

"But I want to help." She turned in his arms and gazed up at his face, handsome in spite of the concern etched there.

He ran his hand up and down her back. "You did help. You gathered the only people who might be able to deal with this situation."

She only hoped it was enough for the ghost battle that was happening right now on the other side of that closed door.

Chapter Thirty-Three

"This damn door is too thick. I can't hear a thing," Natalie grumbled then took a step back from the door that itself had taken on an evil feel to it.

"I for one am grateful it's so thick," Bobby, standing a couple of steps below where she stood on the landing, commented.

"Natalie?!"

The sound of her name being called, not from above but from below had Natalie frowning.

"Was that Harper?" she asked, glancing at Liam.

She didn't wait for an answer but ran down the single flight of stairs and reached for the knob of the door that separated the emergency stairwell from the ninth-floor hallway. She felt an undeniable sense of relief when that knob turned in her hand.

Leaning into the hallway, she saw Harper and Alice by the elevator. "We're down here!"

Harper turned and visibly breathed out a sigh of relief. "Oh, thank God you're all right. We heard at the theater that Letisha is trapped and you were calling for help," she said as she strode fast down the hall, Alice almost jogging behind her to keep up.

"We would've been here sooner but we had to walk. What did we miss?" Alice asked when she finally arrived, perspiring as heavily as she was panting for breath.

"As far as we know, half of the ghosts are upstairs fighting that thing that trapped Letisha and the crew on the tenth floor. But wait. Why did you walk here?" Natalie asked.

"We heard you were in trouble but Sam was all like, *the show must go on. Keep filming.* So we snuck out of the theater," Harper explained.

"I tried to hot wire the van but I couldn't. These vehicles with the new-fangled ignitions aren't as easy to steal as the old ones used to be, so we had to hoof it from there." Alice added.

Hot wire? Steal? Natalie's eyes widened. Who *was* this woman? She had thought she knew Alice but the more she learned the more she realized she knew nothing at all about Alice Mudd.

A bulb overhead in the hallway light fixture exploded, sending shards of thin broken glass falling to the floor. Harper covered her head, ducking into the stairway with Alice on her heels.

Things weren't much better in there. The lights in the stairwell flashed. The fixtures buzzed while noises from above—bumps and crashes—filtered down to them.

Paulina glanced up at the ceiling. "That doesn't seem good."

"No, it does not," Liam agreed, glancing up at the tenth-floor door a flight above them. "Nat, I think we should block the door. We don't want that thing to be able to get out."

"With what?" Natalie asked. "It'll be able to just walk right through whatever we pile in front of the door."

He tipped his head toward the shaker still clutched in her hand. "The salt."

"Oh, right." She turned and ran back up the stairs.

The door at the top was literally vibrating with energy. Could everyone see it or just her?

"Nat. You might want to hurry."

She turned to see Liam standing behind her on the steps and staring at the door.

So not just her then.

Hand shaking, she up-ended the salt shaker and shook, sprinkling it in a faint line across the floor at the bottom of the door as the roar of the indistinguishable sounds surrounding them got louder.

"Babe."

Natalie glanced up and found Liam close, hand extended.

"Give me." He took the salt from her hand, saying, "Pour. There's no time to sprinkle."

He twisted the top off the shaker and poured a thin line along the threshold as the sound of whatever was happening on the other side got more intense.

Sick to her stomach she wished she could do more than pour salt. Her ghost friends were in there. Not to mention the PNC crew, whose lives were in danger all because they'd followed their boss's order.

And of course, there was Letisha. Why would she have risked going after that thing? She wasn't without powers. She'd seen it. Felt it. She should have known better.

"Question. I'm no expert in these matters, but even if you block the door's threshold with salt, can't that thing just come through a wall? Or the ceiling?" Bobby asked, eyeing the line of salt on the floor that admittedly didn't look like much of a deterrent.

Natalie sighed and took a step away from the door,

since it was seeming more and more dangerous to be standing too closely too it. "I don't know, Bobby."

It wasn't a perfect plan, but it was all they had at the moment.

But if they all got out of this thing alive—and *not* possessed by demons—she was going to demand that some useful information on fighting malevolent entities be put on the internet immediately by... somebody.

The door flinging open and crashing against the wall right next to where Liam stood stopped that thought dead in her head.

Then Natalie, and everyone else in that stairwell, stared and waited to see who—or what—was about to come through that doorway.

Chapter Thirty-Four

Letisha, white faced and disheveled, stood on the threshold.

"Watch out for the salt on the floor!" Natalie shouted as Liam held the door open.

Letisha stumbled over the line of salt, narrowly missing breaking it. Paulina gripped Letisha's arms and guided her down a few stairs, where she collapsed onto a step.

The two PNC crew members directly behind Letisha leaped over the salt line and trotted half-way down the stairs. They stopped where Letisha sat blocking their way and turned. Both looked back at the doorway, as if they expected to be followed.

What they didn't know was that they had been. Gabe emerged right behind.

Millie rushed up the stairs to meet him. When they met, Gabe reached for Millie's hand, saying, "Hi."

Fingers entwined, Millie breathed out a relieved sounding, "Hi."

"Where's Harriet?" Natalie asked, concerned when Vinny and Ricky came through but Harriet did not.

Ricky hooked a thumb toward the door. "She's in there talking to that thing."

"She thinks with some counseling it might be able to move on," Gabe explained.

"Is she going to be okay in there with it?" Natalie asked.

Gabe nodded. "The priest stayed with her. He was actually able to subdue it with his holy water and Bible and all those prayers he was shouting."

"I was never much for religion but I might be now after witnessing that," Vinny commented.

Evie took a step forward toward the star. "I'm glad you're all right, you cad."

"Aw, Evie. Would you have missed me if I were gone?" Vinny asked with a perfect leading man smile.

"No. Not at all. I'd be perfectly happy to never see the likes of you again...but I'm still glad."

He smiled broader, but Natalie's attention was drawn away from the bickering movie stars. Letisha, looking pale as she braced one hand on the wall and the other on the railing, stood. She stared in the direction of Gabe and Millie.

"Letisha. You all right?" Natalie asked.

"Maybe you should go to the hospital," Paulina suggested.

"Give her a bourbon," Alice suggested. "She'll be fine."

Liam came down the stairs. "Letisha. Can you tell me how you're feeling? I'm a doctor."

"Oh, right!" Natalie spun to Paulina. "It's okay. Liam's a doctor."

Liam frowned back at Natalie. "What, did you forget?"

"No. Well, yes. Maybe." She cringed.

His dark brows formed into a line above his eyes. "Natalie."

"I'm sorry. But you only work with dead people. It's easy to forget you're a real doctor too. Okay?"

With a huff, he shook his head and turned back to Letisha. "First of all, let's get out of this stairway."

Everyone, living and dead, piled out into the ninth-floor hallway, where Liam stood Letisha beneath one of the unbroken light fixtures and looked into her eyes.

"Are you feeling light-headed?" he asked.

Letisha shook her head. "I—I heard...talking."

"Ah." Liam nodded and glanced over his shoulder. "I think this might be Gabe-induced."

Of course. Letisha wasn't there for the interview with Sam when Gabe and Millie made their public debut. This was her first time experiencing the disembodied voices of the ghosts she couldn't see.

"Gabe." Natalie looked toward her friend and tipped her head toward the medium.

Gabe nodded. Still holding Millie's hand, he said, "Hello, Letisha. My name's Gabe Miller. I was murd—"

Natalie shook her head violently, stopping Gabe mid-sentence. Letisha looked ready to pass out already, without knowing Gabe had been murdered.

"Um, I died last year," he said. "Shortly before Natalie gained the ability to see and hear me. See all of us, actually."

Hand still braced on the wall, Letisha raised her gaze to meet Natalie's. "You weren't lying."

"No, I wasn't." Natalie shook her head. "Gabe is my best friend... Uh, no offense," she added, glancing quickly at Liam and then Harper.

Liam let out a short laugh. "Believe me, I know where I stand with you two."

Harper's face crumpled as she said, "Aw. I love that you and Gabe are best friends."

Oh, boy.

Natalie had a strong feeling all of this was going to end up in Harper's next book. And she'd be lucky if Harper didn't turn it into some weird paranormal love story involving a living and a ghost. Maybe a love triangle. But honestly, she was so grateful her friends were all right, she was okay with that.

Harper writing her story seemed trivial now. How could it be anything but after they'd faced the threat of that malevolent entity? The entity her ghost friends had battled and conquered. All to save her and the rest of the livings involved.

In a state of mental and physical exhaustion from all that had happened, Natalie was extra emotional. The love she had for these ghosts—the ones who were new in her life and the ones she called friends—overwhelmed her.

"I'm glad Gabe and I are best friends too," she said, agreeing with Harper.

She reached out one hand toward Gabe. He extended his own hand toward hers. Their fingertips met—and Gabe's passed right through hers.

"But sometimes I forget we can't actually touch." Natalie let out a short, teary laugh as she pulled her hand back.

"Wait. May I try something?" Letisha asked holding her hand out, palm up.

"Uh, sure. What?" Natalie asked.

"Each of you—Gabe and Natalie—place one of your hands on top of mine."

Natalie's gaze met Gabe's. He shrugged.

"Okay," Natalie said and did as Letisha asked.

So did Gabe. And for the first time, they didn't pass right through each other.

It wasn't cold air she felt. This time, she could swear she felt the warmth of Gabe's flesh. The rough callouses on the palm of his hand as it faced hers.

"Oh my God," she gasped. She raised her gaze to his. "I can feel your hand."

"I can feel yours too," he said, holding on to Millie so they all heard.

"How does this work?" Natalie asked Letisha.

"I didn't know if it would. Sometimes I can feel them, they touch me, but I wasn't sure it would transfer to you."

"This is amazing. Can I hug him too? If I keep hold of your hand?" Natalie asked.

"I don't know." Letisha shrugged. "Give it a try."

Natalie took a step closer and reached out her other arm, wrapping it around Gabe. She felt his arm wrap around her.

"Oh my God. We're hugging. Millie, Liam, get in here too," Natalie said.

Millie joined the hug fest while Liam shook his head. "Yeah. I'm good over here. Thanks." But he was smiling while he said it.

Finally, after she didn't know how long, it seemed ridiculous to be standing there hugging. Silent. Connected through Letisha's power as everyone watched.

Natalie pulled back and turned to the woman who'd been her mortal enemy a day ago. "Letisha. I don't know how to thank you. This... It was such a gift."

Letisha let out a huff. "No. Your ability—being able to see and hear them—that's a true gift."

Natalie considered that. "I love the spirits I've gotten to know. Truly I do. You guys know that, right?"

Gabe and Millie nodded.

"But this ability?" Natalie continued. "Most of the time it doesn't feel like a gift."

Letisha raised her gaze to the ceiling and shook her head. "Why is the power always given to those who don't appreciate it?"

Natalie cringed. "I am sorry."

"It's all right. I make do with what I have. But if

you're ever looking to expand into the psychic medium space, let me know. I'd be happy to take on an apprentice."

A laugh burst out of Natalie. "I'm not planning on it, but thanks."

"Why are you not filming?" Sam demanded from down the hall.

In the midst of the emotions, Natalie hadn't heard the elevator doors open. But Sam had indeed arrived and was looking angrily at her crew. Jake the cameraman in particular.

Alice glanced around at the group of livings. "All those in favor of sending Sam upstairs to see the tenth floor, say aye."

Chapter Thirty-Five

"Nat! Wake up. It's Halloween!"

Natalie groaned and resisted the urge to pull the sheet over her head. It was bad enough the pipes had been fixed and the cast were back sleeping at the theater. She didn't need a ghost waking her up when she'd finally fallen into a deep sleep.

"Gabe," she groaned. "You're like a kid on Christmas morning, I swear. It's just Halloween."

"Which is *the* big holiday in the ghost community. You know this." He let out a huff.

"Yes. I know. I'm getting up. I promise."

"Why are you talking?" Harper moaned from the next bed over.

"Because Gabe is talking to me."

Harper groaned. "I think I liked it better when you hid you could talk to them."

"Somebody's cranky this morning," Gabe commented, which luckily Harper couldn't hear. "This might help—tell her the caterers just delivered breakfast and brewed a giant urn of fresh coffee. Everyone's over there sniffing it now."

Natalie smiled, knowing that by *everyone* Gabe meant the ghosts, who truly embraced their ability to smell since they'd lost the ability to eat.

"Gabe says there's breakfast and fresh coffee," Natalie repeated temptingly.

"I'm up. I'm up," Alice said, swinging her feet over the edge of the bed while rubbing her eyes.

"Fine. I'll get up," Harper said. "What time is it?"

Natalie glanced at Gabe. "Eleven a.m.," he supplied.

"Eleven," Natalie repeated.

"Nooo! Why?" Harper laid back down and covered her face with the sheet. "We don't film the live episode until eight tonight."

"But the ghosts are putting on their show for us at noon," Natalie said, talking to Harper through the sheet.

"Putting on a show for *you*, you mean. I won't be able to see or hear it," Harper grumbled.

"Actually, Bobby says people can hear Clara sing and play the piano. It's one of the ways she enjoys freaking out the livings," Gabe supplied.

Natalie's eyes widened. "Ooo, really? That is interesting."

"What's interesting?" Harper asked, flipping the covers back down.

"You might be able to hear the little girl ghost."

"Ooo, really?" Harper sat up, looking more interested.

"I think we got her attention." Gabe smiled.

"Looks like. Now go away. I need to get dressed," Natalie said, shooing Gabe out of the room.

Besides, Alice had just shuffled into the bathroom and Gabe definitely didn't want to be in the vicinity for that.

"All right. I'm going. But don't be late. And Bobby said to tell you to wear something nice. This is a *classy theater*. His words," Gabe relayed.

Natalie rolled her eyes. "I'll see what I can do."

An hour later, she was dressed, fed and ready for the show. Liam was there too, having driven over from the hotel. He'd threatened and bull dozed his way past the unfortunate crew member who'd dared to think he should try to block Liam's entrance into the Stanley.

As they waited to be seated, Harper and Alice stood alongside Natalie and Liam, looking skeptical.

Finally Alice asked, "What are we waiting for? Do we have assigned seats? Do I need a ticket?"

Natalie smiled. "No Alice, no ticket. We're just waiting for the usher to seat us."

Horace, who still took his job as usher at the Stanley very seriously, was currently leading a group of local Utica spirits to their seats.

There was a queue of more ghosts—who'd mostly ignored Natalie and the rest of the livings—waiting to be seated behind them, but her group was next in line to be seated.

Alice glanced around them then leaned in and whispered, "A ghost usher?"

"Yes, Alice. His name is Horace. He's been an usher here since the year the theater opened right about the time the Great Depression started."

"Do her answers about ghosts always come with a history lesson?" Alice asked Liam.

Liam nodded. "Pretty much, but it's usually accompanied by some century old murder evidence."

"That reminds me!" Natalie spun to face Liam. "We still have to talk about Evie and Vinny's murders. There should be something written about it in the local paper's archives, right? Even if it was almost a hundred years ago."

"See what I mean?" Liam said to Alice. Meanwhile Harper had whipped out a notebook and pen and begun scribbling rapidly, no doubt taking notes on the conversation for her book.

"It's amazing you've lasted with her this long," Alice mumbled to Liam, hooking a thumb in Natalie's direction..

Natalie didn't have time to deal with the insult because Horace was back.

It was time to take their seats.

"Horace, do you know where my friends are? The ghosts from Mudville."

"Yes, ma'am. They're seated up front. Please, follow me," Horace said with the sweep of one arm.

How formal. She kind of loved it.

"Okay." Natalie smiled and glanced back at the others. "Follow him."

Harper lowered her notebook and raised her brows at that command but they all followed Natalie as she followed Horace.

Walking into the theater, dressed in the best outfit she had with her, and seeing the rows filled with people, even if they were ghosts, Natalie could imagine the theater back in its glory days in the years following its opening. When stars like Evie and Vinny walked the red carpet. When patrons donned their best clothing, gathered their saved pennies and splurged on a night out at the theater in an attempt to forget, if only for a couple of hours, the devastating economic depression that was crippling the country.

Horace paused by a half empty row down near the front and extended on arm.

Natalie turned to the others. "These are our seats," she said.

"All righty. So glad there was room for us," Alice said snarkily.

To Alice, the theater looked empty. But to Natalie, it looked like it was going to be a near sellout crowd after Horace finished seating all those in the line in the lobby.

"All right." Liam nodded and started into the row.

When he reached the fourth seat in, Natalie said, "Stop!"

He glanced back, brow raised.

"Don't go any farther. You can sit right there. One seat over and you'll be sitting in Ricky's lap."

Liam shook his head but settled into the seat she'd indicated, before saying in the vicinity of the seat to his left, "Hello, Ricky."

"Hey, man," Ricky replied even though Liam wouldn't hear him.

Natalie smiled, knowing being with her wasn't easy for Liam, but also knowing it certainly wasn't boring.

She followed Liam into the row, and Harper slid in behind her, no doubt leaving Alice purposely with the aisle seat. After this week, they all knew she'd be up at least once to use the restroom during the show.

Once they were all settled, Natalie leaned in front of Liam. "Hi, Ricky. Hi, Harriet. Where are Millie and Gabe?"

Harriet leaned forward to say, "It's a surprise."

A surprise?

"Okay," Natalie said, leaning back. What in the world could they have planned?

"I hope you're going to tell me what's happening on stage since I can't see or hear anything," Harper commented.

"You might be surprised," Ricky said to Natalie, leaning forward to shoot her a grin.

"I will," Natalie told Harper as she wondered what the ghosts had in store for them all.

The lights went down and the heavy red curtains opened to reveal the movie screen.

"What is this?" Liam asked.

"I have no idea," Natalie whispered.

They didn't have long to wait as a flickering light lit the screen and the opening credits of a black and white film appeared.

Natalie gasped, surprised and delighted as she read the credits. "It's Evie and Vinny's film," she whispered.

But that wasn't the only surprise as Gabe and Millie, holding hands, walked to center stage. "Good afternoon and happy Halloween!" Gabe said, loud and clear as the theater exploded into ghostly applause.

Liam drew back. "That was unexpected."

"No kidding," she whispered as she joined in the applause.

Harper and Alice, still new at being able to hear Gabe, followed Natalie's lead and clapped along as well, even as they looked slightly terrified.

When the applause died down, Natalie stopped clapping. Harper did as well, but good old Alice kept going. A few ghosts chuckled nearby as Natalie reached over and stilled Alice's hands with her own.

"I'm Gabe. This lovely lady next to me is Millie, and we're your hosts for today's show."

Another spattering of ghostly applause erupted. This time Natalie did not participate, not wanting to send Alice into another round of uncontrolled applause.

"You might have noticed we've been joined by

some livings today." Gabe indicated Natalie's row, but then swept an arm upward toward the mezzanine.

Natalie twisted and looked up to see the entire cast and crew, including Sam, seated in the front row of the mezzanine level. Yet another surprise.

"Today, we'll be treated to snippets of a classic film starring the Stanley Theater's very own Evie Hartwell and Vincent Carlisle." The two actors ran onto the stage with a curtsey and a bow to renewed applause.

When it died down, Gabe continued, "While the film plays, the actors themselves will perform along in front of the big screen. A little something for both the living and the dead to watch. Enjoy!"

Gabe led Millie off to the side, but Evie and Vinny remained.

Movie music swelled, filling the theater as the film, which had been edited to something like a highlight reel, switched to a dramatic scene between Evie and Vinny.

In the film they were enemies, fighting in an emotional scene that culminated in the end with a movie worthy kiss between them. As the movie showed them larger than life on the big screen, the actors performed the scene exactly on the stage, right down to the kiss at the end.

They both took a bow as the scene ended and the applause erupted.

The film switched to a scene where a band played. On the stage, Vinny extended his hand to Evie just as he did on the screen. Then the two began to dance to the music, performing a beautiful ballroom routine. The couple on stage mirrored the on-screen couple step-by-step to perfection.

At the conclusion of the dance, closing credits ran on the screen as the actors received a standing ovation from the audience. This time, Natalie did join in, standing along with the rest.

Then Gabe was back with Millie. "Thank you, Evie and Vinny. What an amazing performance, but you haven't seen anything yet. There's a lot more show left, folks. Next up, please welcome the Stanley's own writer in residence. Playwright Harold Ludlow will do a dramatic reading of one of his original works, which will be captioned on the screen behind me for the livings to be able to read and follow along. Harold Ludlow."

Words appeared on the screen as Harold took the stage. His original work turned out to be an exceptionally lengthy soliloquy which had Liam fidgeting in his seat next to her and Alice snoring on the aisle.

Finally the piece ended and the screen went dark as Harold took a bow.

Next to Natalie, Liam mumbled, "Thank God."

The polite applause from the livings woke Alice, as Gabe and Millie reappeared on stage. "Thank you, Harold, for that moving piece. Now for our next performer, please welcome to the stage child prodigy Clara Delaney."

Clara skipping onto the stage and settled on the bench of the piano revealed when the movie screen rose into the ceiling and out of site.

She was so small, her feet barely reached the pedals of the grand piano. But when she set her fingers to the keys and began to play, beautiful music filled the theater.

Next to her Harper gasped and Liam squeezed her hand. Natalie glanced at him as he turned to look at her.

"What?" she asked.

"I can hear the music," he said.

"Me too," Harper whispered.

Amazed, Natalie smiled. "I'm so glad."

Meanwhile, Clara performed beautifully, a true professional in spite of her age. She finished the song on the piano and then stood, moving to center stage to tap dance while singing acapella.

Liam gripped Natalie's hand even tighter.

"You hear singing and tap?" Natalie guessed.

He nodded staring at what to him would appear to be an empty stage.

Poor Liam. He was getting a lot of new ghostly experience thrown at him this trip. Harper too. Meanwhile, Alice seemed to be enjoying every moment. As if this was any old normal show.

Clara finished, took a bow, stuck her tongue out at Natalie, then ran off stage.

"Kids will be kids, am I right? But wasn't she talented, folks?" Gabe asked, really getting into his role as host.

When the applause died down, Gabe visibly sobered. "Before we move on to the final act of the show, I did want to acknowledge some people who've made this all possible. First and foremost, Sam and the crew from the Paranormal Channel. When they heard we wanted to put on a show for the livings as well as the spirit community, they went above and beyond, using their technological resources to bring you this amazing event."

Mixed feeling about Sam and her show aside, Natalie had to give credit where credit was due. She stood and turned to face Sam and the crew in the mezzanine while applauding as loudly as she could.

When she turned back to face the front, Gabe said, "Stay standing, Natalie."

She froze, eyes wide. "Um, why?"

"Because we'd all would like to thank you." Gabe waved to someone in the wings.

Suddenly the stage was crowded with the Stanley ghosts she'd come to know and love. Bobby, Evie, Vinny, even Clara and the ghost priest came to stand next to Gabe and Millie.

"Natalie Chase, you and your power to communicate with us has affected every one of us. And that is why we'd all like to dedicate this final number to you." Gabe glanced at Clara who scampered back to the piano.

She set her little hands on the keys but the first notes came not from the piano, but from Millie, who began to sing,

"Now won't you listen, honey, while I say. How could you tell me that you're going away..."

"Wow. Millie can really sing," Natalie whispered.

"What is this song? I love it," Harper asked.

"*After You've Gone*, Marion Harris, nineteen eighteen," Harriet supplied from a few seats down.

Natalie passed that information on to Harper.

"Don't say we must part. Don't break your baby's

heart..." Millie continued while Clara joined in with the piano.

By the end of the song everyone on stage was singing along. Even Bobby, Gabe and the priest.

And when the first song ended they rolled right into a rousing group rendition of *Ain't We Got Fun*.

"Everyone, sing along," Gabe encouraged. "You know the words!"

Alice didn't need to be told twice. She was clapping and singing—only slightly off key—as loud as she could. Even Liam sang a verse.

When the song ended the joint living and spirit applause was nearly deafening.

Natalie could swear she felt it vibrating the building. But that was okay, because she'd never felt such a positive energy surrounding her. As intense as the negative energy had been from the entity, only this was all light and love and happiness.

She glanced up at the mezzanine. Even Letisha was smiling.

Natalie caught Sam's eye and tipped her head to acknowledge the woman's contribution to this amazing event.

Finally, after the performers had left the stage after taking two curtain calls, Alice turned and said, "That was the best show I've seen in a long time. We need to do this every year."

Natalie laughed but it wasn't such a bad idea.

Chapter Thirty-Six

"A free show. Free champagne. Free hors d'oeuvres. This is my kinda party," Alice said outside in the lobby. "Too bad there's only a handful of us to enjoy it."

Natalie glanced around. There might only be a handful of livings, as Alice had said—the cast and crew only put them at a little over a dozen people—but the lobby was teeming with spirits.

Most of the guests who'd come to the show had stayed for the after party. It was wall to wall in there, which made it hard to navigate for Natalie who could actually see the obstacles in her path.

Alice, on the other hand, had barreled right through a good dozen ghosts in her path to the champagne.

"Miss Chase."

At the sound of her name, Natalie turned to find a woman reaching out to touch her sleeve. She resisted the urge to shiver from the ghostly touch and said, "Yes. That's me."

"I'm Roberta. I used to work here at the Stanley, cleaning. I was here the night Miss Hartwell and Mr. Carlisle died."

"You were?" Natalie gripped Liam's arm tightly with excitement.

He glanced down on her claw-like hold on him. "I'm assuming something is happening."

"Yes. There's a woman who was here the night Evie and Vinny were murdered."

"Hmm. Well, let me know if you need me. Harper and I are going to be over here watching Alice fill her purse with shrimp while not hearing or seeing anything that you are."

Fine. She'd work this case on her own. Turning back to Roberta, Natalie said, "What can you tell me about that night?"

"It was just like any other night... except for the gifts."

"The gifts?" Natalie asked.

"Yes. Usually whenever Miss Hartwell was at the theater, she received all sorts of things from gentlemen admirers. Champagne, flowers, even perfume and jewelry. Often times I was asked to bring the gifts back since patrons aren't allowed backstage or in the dressing rooms. But this night was different."

"How?" Natalie asked, heart pounding.

"Mr. Carlisle received a gift this time. A man asked me to deliver a box of chocolates to his dressing room, which I thought was rather odd."

"And did you do it?"

"I did. And that night, both Mr. Carlisle and Miss Hartwell were found dead in their dressing rooms. It was horrible. We were all shaken up. After they took the bodies away we—the staff—just sat here waiting for the police to interview us and crying. When my turn came they asked me where the champagne came from, because they found glasses of it in both Mr. Carlisle and Miss Hartwell's dressing room. They thought that must be the connection. What had killed them both since it was the only thing they both had that we could see. This was right after Prohibition had been repealed, so the spirits were flowing again but this champagne wasn't cheap. Not everyone had bottles of it, you know? I told them a bottle had been delivered to Miss Hartwell. They took it as evidence and I was told not to clean the dressing rooms in case there was more evidence in there."

"And did they find poison in the champagne?" Natalie asked.

"No. They were stumped but the theater had to get back to business so they told me to go ahead and clean out the dressing rooms. That's when I found the box of chocolates that I had delivered to Mr. Carlisle was in Miss Hartwell's dressing room. And two pieces were missing."

"Did you tell the police?" Natalie asked.

She shook her head.

"Why not?"

"I'm too embarrassed to say."

"Please, Roberta. What you know could solve two murders."

The ghost drew in a breath. "I didn't tell the police because I took the chocolates home and ate them myself."

Natalie gasped. "And you died. Because the chocolates were poisoned, not the champagne."

Roberta nodded.

"Oh my God. Roberta, do you remember who gave you those chocolates to put in Vincent's dressing room?"

She nodded.

"Who?"

She turned to look around the room... and then

pointed at Edgar Winslow. The man who spent every performance of his life and afterlife in the back row seat in which he'd died.

"Edgar Winslow?" Natalie asked. "You're sure?"

Roberta nodded. "Definitely. He was much younger then, of course, but he was here for every show. And he always sent something back for Miss Hartwell when she was in town. He was quite her admirer."

"But this one time he sent a gift to Vincent instead. A poisoned gift, not anticipating Vinny would share it with Evie."

"Eddie killed me?" Evie said.

Natalie spun and found the starlet behind her, hand clutched to her chest.

"What's this?" Bobby asked, moving closer.

"Did you just say Winslow killed you?" Vincent came closer as well.

"Killed *us*," Evie corrected.

"It was the chocolate that was poisoned, not the champagne. Edgar had it delivered to Vinny's dressing room," Natalie supplied, as more ghosts heard the conversation and began to gather.

"Why?" Vinny asked.

"Jealousy," Evie supplied.

Vinny shook his head. "But there was nothing going on between us. At least not back then."

Not back then... Natalie's brows rose. Did that mean there was something going on between the two stars now? Interesting, but a tidbit for later.

Evie flicked one wrist. "He couldn't know that. You remember how we played things up for the movie premiere. The studio said it would sell tickets. Eddie sent me gifts all the time. Expensive things. He was definitely sweet on me. There was nothing going on between us, of course. Not only because he was married, but because a smart girl knows to play hard to get."

"But he's been here right under your noses the entire time. Did you two never talk after he died?" Natalie asked.

"Darling, I died in 1933. Eddie didn't join our ghost ranks here until close to fifty years later. And no, he never talked to me. As I said, there was never anything between us except for the gifts, and he wasn't the only male admirer I had. I didn't think anything of it."

"But now what?" Natalie asked. "I mean, he intentionally murdered Vinny and was responsible for the deaths of both Evie and Roberta. He can't just get away with it."

It seemed to her they had a big problem. What did they do about a murderer who was a ghost?

"Oh, he won't get away with it," Bobby said. "Look."

Two ghosts, in police uniforms, were currently hauling Edgar Winslow out of the theater.

"What's going on? Is there some kind of a ghost jail?" Natalie asked.

"Not exactly. But he will be banished from the theater and everywhere else around here. He'll have to live out the rest of eternity alone. Not a perfect justice system but it's all we've got." Bobby shrugged.

Vinny wrapped one arm around Evie as they both watched Edgar being forcibly removed. Evie turned under Vinny's arm to face him.

"I can't believe it. After all these years we finally know what happened. And it was your fault, you big lug! You always blamed me." Evie slapped Vinny's chest.

He caught her hand, hauled her close and pressed a screen-worthy kiss against her mouth. Finally releasing her, he said, "Shut up and marry me."

"What?" Evie squeaked.

"You heard me. Let's get married. Look, we've even got a priest. Why not? You got a better offer?" Vinny asked.

Evie drew in a breath and let it out, finally saying, "What the hell. All right. I'll marry you."

Natalie couldn't help but laugh. "I thought you two hated each other."

Evie waved that notion away. "Darling, enemies to lovers has always been my favorite trope."

Natalie smiled. "Yeah. It's mine too."

She felt Liam's arm around her shoulders and glanced up.

"What's happening?" he asked.

She shook her head. "You wouldn't believe me if I told you."

Chapter Thirty-Seven

"Doctor Finch, has your time on *Halloween Ghost Challenge* changed your opinion about the existence of the supernatural?"

"Not one bit."

"But you heard actual ghosts during your time here."

"There is a phenomenon known as mass hallucination where a group of people in close proximity will experience the same delusion simultaneously. That's what I believed happened here."

"Tiffany, can you tell us how *Halloween Ghost Challenge* has changed your life?"

"Oh my God. So when we got our cell phones back after we wrapped there was a message from my agent and they want me for the next season of *Big Brother*!"

"Congratulations. What from your experience on this show will you take with you to your next endeavor?"

"Um, I don't know. Working nights sucks so that's going in my contract from now on. And I'll never appear on a show with a woman who can talk to ghosts again. Total scene stealer."

"You're referring to Madame Letisha."

"Hell, no. I meant Natalie."

* * *

"Derek, how have your millions of YouTube followers responded to your time on *Halloween Ghost Challenge*?"

"They all thought it was totally gnarly. And I got a sponsor who wants me to do more ghost investigations and stuff. I'm thinking of asking Natalie if she wants to partner up with me."

"Do you think she'd accept your offer?"

"She probably would, except for that big scary boyfriend of hers."

"You could ask Madame Letisha to be your partner for the investigation... Derek, why are you laughing?"

"Megan, you came to the *Halloween Ghost Challenge* as a self-proclaimed super fan of Madame Letisha and now do I understand you're going to be working with her?"

"Yes. I'm so excited. Madame Letisha has agreed to take me on as an assistant. She's such an amazing talent."

"While on the show did you get to spend any time with Natalie Chase?"

"In my opinion, compared to Madame Letisha Natalie Chase is a complete fraud."

"Madame Letisha, now that the show has wrapped, what are your feelings about your fellow ghost whisperer, Natalie Chase?"

"Natalie? She does have a certain amount of raw talent, but she is, of course, beyond a doubt a complete amateur. In this business there is no substitute for the kind of experience I bring to the profession. I believe that was evident when I single-handedly took on the dark entity at the hotel."

"Doctor Walsh..."

"You can still call me Liam. And I still don't know why you want to talk to me. I wasn't on the show."

"Do you regret not being part of this season's cast of *Halloween Ghost House*?"

"Yes, I do."

"And why is that?"

"Because you people and your show almost got my girlfriend killed, that's why."

"Um, Doctor Walsh? You're still wired. Liam! Can you please come back and leave us your microphone?"

"Natalie--"

"Hi. Is this going to take long? The ghosts need to be back in Mudville before midnight."

"What happens if they're not?"

"We don't know for sure but I'm not about to find out."

"All right. We'll be quick. Tell us, now that the show is wrapped, what one thing will you take away from the experience?"

"One thing? How can I choose just one thing? I mean, tonight's impromptu ghost wedding is up there, of course. But I'll never forget facing that dark entity for as long as I live. But oh, the ghost show—that was beyond amazing. I think if I had to choose just one thing, it would be all the wonderful new friends I met here in Utica."

"You mean Letisha and your fellow cast members?"

"Um..."

"You were speaking about the ghosts, weren't you?"

"Yeah. I was. Sorry."

Epilogue

Natalie stood in the center of the meeting room and looked around her. "This old depot has never looked so good, if I do say so myself."

"Actually, this train station looked pretty good a hundred years ago. But you are right, I don't think it was ever decorated for the holidays this beautifully," Harriet said, standing next to Natalie. "I am sorry I couldn't help."

Natalie waved away her concern. "Are you serious? You probably saved all our lives with that entity at the hotel."

"The priest did more than I did."

"That's not what I heard. He said he subdued it but you're the reason it moved on."

"All I did was reason with it. Tell it that the facility

had been shut down and the people responsible for his abuse and death punished. It seems that was his unfinished business so he moved on." Harriet shrugged, as if it was nothing.

Natalie, having felt the power of that thing, knew what Harriet had done was definitely something.

"You're being modest. And, who says you didn't help with the decorations? You told me when I had the tree straight in the stand. You handled the ghost guest list invitations. And most importantly, you came and warned me when the cat was chewing on the light cord."

Having a ghost bat in the shop was enough. She didn't need to have the ghost of Mr. Darcy the cat haunting her for the rest of her life because he'd gotten himself electrocuted.

Harriet smiled. "Happy to do it, and look. Your guests are starting to arrive."

Natalie's first giant Christmas gathering in Mudville was about to begin.

The invitation list was vast. Harper, Stone, Agnes, and Alice were on it. As well as the members of the ghost council. And there was an open invitation for anyone else who was in town for the holiday and didn't have other plans to stop by for a drink and a nibble.

Natalie had set out one long table in the meeting

room, covered with charcuterie boards and bottles of wine. She did own a wine shop, after all.

She also owned a bookshop and every guest tonight was to take home a book. Her gift to them.

The books were piled on a side table wrapped in brown paper and tied with twine, decorated with a sprig of pine and holly.

On the wrapping was written nothing but a sentence—the slightest hint of what the book was about. Other than that, the guests would have to choose blindly, and hopefully be surprised and delighted by what they'd chosen when they got home.

But the thing that made the biggest impact in the meeting room was the twelve foot tall—and probably almost as wide—fresh cut Christmas tree provided by Stone's family farm.

It was the kind of tree Natalie had always wanted when she'd lived in the city but could never have. Just like this was the kind of party she'd always wanted to throw.

And as she looked at the table filled shoulder to shoulder with her friends both living and dead, seated side by side, she realized she finally had the friends she didn't realize she'd been missing until moving here.

"Having fun?" Liam asked, coming up behind

where she stood and wrapping his arms around her waist.

"Yes. I do wish the Utica ghosts could have been here though."

"You know, we can go and visit. It's not that far."

"You'd do that? Come with me?" She turned in his arms and met his gaze.

"Of course, I would."

"You're getting pretty good about all the ghost stuff," she observed. "Much better than when you first learned about them."

Liam bobbed his head to one side. "They're not so bad, once you get to know them. And I do have to say, the ghosts make excellent party guests. They don't eat or drink. There's nothing to clean up afterward. If I could just see where they are so I stop walking through them, we'd be good."

"Hold that thought." Natalie disengaged herself from Liam's embrace and ran to the Christmas tree.

Bending down she grabbed a badly wrapped package, which was not her fault. Not everything was as easy to wrap as a book.

Trotting back to where Liam waited, she thrust the package at him. "Merry Christmas, one day early."

"What is this?" he asked.

"Open it, silly, and see."

"All right." That dimple was back. Liam might try to act like a grump but deep down he was a big old softie.

Tearing into the paper, he pulled out a pair of thermal goggles.

"You can see if those help. I'm not sure they'll work but thermal imaging is supposed to show ghosts."

He turned the goggles over in his hand. "Where did you get these?"

"Don't judge me, but they might have accidentally fallen into my bag in Utica." She cringed.

Liam laughed. "That's my girl."

"Doctor Walsh. Are you encouraging my petty theft?"

"They owe you more than whatever those cost. Considering you got paid next to nothing for risking your life for that show, which had the highest ratings on PNC in the last two years, I'd say the people at the network are the ones who made out like bandits."

"You're right. I won't feel guilty. Oh, speaking of thieves—did I ever tell you that Alice knows how to hot wire a car?"

Liam shook his head. "No, but I'm not at all surprised. It's a shame you didn't find her grandmother in the graveyard. Can you imagine what that old bird would have been like?"

Natalie laughed. "I know, right? Though it's a good thing she's not there. It means she passed on."

And one quirky old bird in her life was enough.

Speaking of Alice... As if on cue she pushed her chair back from the table and stood, though that didn't put her more than a head higher than those who remained seated.

Tapping her glass with a spoon, she began once the room had quieted, "So PNC is looking for a location for the next season of *Ghost Challenge*. And maybe this time, since Natalie is a famous ghost whisperer now and all, they'll choose Mudville."

"Alice. No." Harper looked horrified. "One malevolent encounter was enough for me."

"Wimp." Alice scowled at Harper then turned to Natalie. "Nat? What do you say? If they pick Mudville this time, are you in?"

Things around there had changed a bit since Natalie had been outed on the show. She couldn't deny that. But all of it hadn't been bad.

Business certainly had picked up. Not just for her in the shop, but for the whole town. And so far the tourists hadn't made life unbearable as she feared they might.

Natalie glanced at Gabe, who was in a much happier mood since he and Millie had made an agreement with Harper and Agnes that they could reside in the spare guest room as long as they promised not to go into Harper or Agnes's bedrooms.

Gabe lifted one shoulder in a noncommittal shrug.

She looked back at Liam, who said, "That's completely up to you, babe."

Natalie turned back and with a smile said, "You know what, Alice. Yeah. Sure. I think it might be fun."

WHAT ARE NATALIE, LIAM AND GABE UP TO?
THERE'S MORE GHOSTS, MORE MURDER AND
MORE MUDVILLE MAYHEM IN
CADAVER LAB: GRAVE'S ANATOMY

Dear Reader,

The Cadaver Lab books have quickly become my favorite things to write. Not just because of the fun fantasy of what might happen if livings and ghosts could live side by side, but also because of all the research and things I've learned while writing them.

This book was no exception. Expanding the realm from Mudville and branching out to set part of the story in Utica, New York was a fascinating endeavor. Little did I know when I started that location would be so ripe with ghost stories.

It began when I saw an article about Utica's real life Stanley Theater and its ghosts. But as it turns out, the theater was tame compared to the nearby Hotel Utica, which has quite a history of its own.

More research into the area revealed even more local ghost stories. As it turned out, too many to incorporate in the scope of this story.

So what in the story is real and what did I make up?

Ghost investigations have been conducted on both properties—the hotel and the theater—and EVPs (that's electronic voice phenomena) captured in both.

One employee of the theater spoke of the recently passed "Art, a former projector operator" and he might be the source of the mysterious whistling heard there. But the double murders and the entire cast of ghost characters in the theater, even Bobby LaRue, are my fictional creation.

As for the hotel—where do I begin?

It was built to be and operated as a grand hotel, visited by all the famous people Sam tells us about in the story, from presidents to entertainers to sports icons to adventurers. And its bar was the location of the first beer to be legally served after the repeal of Prohibition.

Sadly, the hotel closed in 1972 and for thirty years after that the building was used as an adult facility. And yes, that facility was closed down for mistreatment of patients.

But I am happy to report investors bought the

building and have restored it to its former glory as a successful operating hotel—except for the tenth through thirteenth floor, which did remain unrenovated and off limits to the public.

Regarding the hotel's spirits, people have reported seeing the ghost of a man in a tuxedo in the bar and a woman in a ball gown on the mezzanine. EVPs of the forbidden upper floors yielded the voice of a nurse and a doctor. But I made up the malevolent entity as well as all the wandering ghosts of the patients.

My sincerest apologies to the hotel for taking creative liberties with their location, which I know is a lovely ghost-free place that I encourage everyone to visit. (Please don't sue me!)

As for some of the other details, the research Liam discusses on brain damage from low level blasts is real and promising. And Sybil Ludington, though not a ghost as far as I know, died in 1839 in Unadilla, New York, the real town that inspired Mudville and she really did make that critical ride during the war when she was just sixteen, as described.

 *Cat*

Spirited Encounters

A SPIRITED SHENANIGANS BONUS READ

"It's just for one night."

"It's *Utica*."

A stack of new releases in her hand, Natalie paused on her way to the front of the book shop and glanced back. "And? So? Liam, I've been there before."

Her tall dark and handsome boyfriend nodded. "Exactly. That's the problem. Remember last time?"

"I don't know what you're worried about." She avoided direct eye contact with his piercing green-eyed gaze as she stopped at the front table just inside the entrance.

He followed her. Moving so he was in her line of sight, he scoffed. "What am I worried about? You almost *died* in Utica."

"What? No, I didn't," she denied and continued to

place the books in what she hoped would be a compelling—and lucrative—display to lure shoppers into the book and wine shop where they'd part with their money and increase her business's bottom line.

His eyes narrowed as he took a step closer. "Are you pretending you don't remember what happened there or are you experiencing short-term memory loss from when you got electrocuted?"

Reaching out, he cupped her face in one big, warm palm, angled her chin up and peered deeply into her eyes.

It would all have been very romantic... *if* he weren't a doctor who'd recently been awarded a grant to research brain damage.

At this point, Natalie was convinced Liam viewed everyone as a case study. Walking, talking, brains on legs. Including her. Maybe she shouldn't judge him too harshly. He worked with cadavers in his lab, which had to make the concept of a live case study extra intriguing.

In any case, there was no doubt that in the middle of their conversation about her going to Utica, Liam had switched from overprotective boyfriend to research doctor mode.

He was still sexy as hell but she wasn't in the mood

to be analyzed for his research. Nor was she going to be told where she could or *could not* go.

She was an adult. She loved Liam but he was not the boss of her—and he was being overly concerned over nothing. Or at least *almost* nothing.

Whatever. She was going.

She scoffed at his questioning her memory function. "I remember perfectly well that I did not *almost die* in Utica. Not even close. I did, however, actually die right here in Mudville. At least, I was technically dead when my heart stopped for three and a half minutes. You might remember that, since you're the hero who brought me back to life with your doctorly CPR skills. But looking at the facts, I'd dare say Mudville with its deadly downed power lines is far more dangerous than Utica."

He returned her scoff. "I beg to differ."

"Agree to disagree," she quipped off handedly, but Liam wasn't having it.

He pinned her with a stormy gaze. "Natalie, you were *chased* by a *demon* through the halls of the hotel in Utica."

She held up one finger to interrupt and correct him. "No. We only *guessed* it was a demonic presence, but as it turns out, it wasn't."

"Natalie," he huffed, his growing frustration clear.

"Just being near that thing brought you to your knees. You couldn't breathe. Don't deny it. Harper and Alice were both there to witness it."

She dismissed his concern with the flick of a wrist. "Yes, but after that I was fine. It was all a misunderstanding. He was just a disgruntled spirit who has since resolved his feelings and moved on to... to wherever it is spirits move on to. He's not even there at the Hotel Utica anymore."

"The hotel that operated as a hospital for years before being shut down for gross mistreatment of patients and then reopened as a hotel again. You can't tell me there's only *one* disgruntled spirit hanging around there." Shaking his head, he folded his arms over his chest.

She was momentarily distracted by her boyfriend's bulging arm muscles before focusing back on her rebuttal to his latest point.

"I'm not even going to be at that hotel. I'll be nowhere near it. I booked a room at the other hotel in town. And the fundraiser is being held in the train station. Besides, I have to go. I already told the historical society I'd come."

"Call them back and tell them you can't."

"You know I hate talking on the phone."

"Then email," he returned.

"Liam, I can't do that. I'm a guest speaker."

"They'll live."

"They already promoted that I'd be there. The least I can do is go and help them raise some money."

He scowled. "Fine. They want money? I'll write them a check."

"That's very generous of you, and yes, you should. But it's not the same thing. They think my being there will help sell event tickets. Raise awareness. You know, get people in the door."

"Because you're a celebrity now?" He cocked his dark brows high.

"I didn't say that, but... yes." She felt her cheeks warm. This new-found—and unwanted— fame was in direct conflict with her introvert nature.

Being on that ghost hunter show filmed at the Stanley Theater in Utica had destroyed any anonymity she'd had before. Completely tossed out the window all she'd done to hide her new ability as a ghost whisperer from everyone in her life except Liam.

But when considering all the attention she'd received since then—both good and bad but all of it unwelcome—this invitation wasn't horrible. Seriously, she was going to be a featured guest at a fancy black tie fundraising event in the gorgeous historic train station just an hour and a half away in Utica.

Heck, it might even be fun.

She'd lead a ghost tour of the train station, give the guests a good show, enjoy a cocktail or two and, hopefully, some tasty hors d'oeuvres, then be home the next morning.

Simple.

Apparently, Liam didn't agree. He still scowled as he said, "Send Alice. The old bird is as big a 'celebrity' as you are. Or get Harper to go. She was a best-selling author even before that ghost show you were all on together."

She had to admit, his use of air quotes around the word *celebrity* hurt a bit, but she moved past it. "It's not the same and you know it."

"Because you can talk to ghosts and they can't?"

"Yes. The organizers want me to lead a ghost tour. But besides that, Harper is traveling for some book thing. And Alice is... well, Alice."

The quirky octogenarian with no verbal filter or social compunctions had spawned more than one viral meme since her memorable appearance on the show.

After proclaiming on video her love of Gas-X, and demonstrating nightly why she needed it, Alice had become internet famous—or was the word *infamous* more accurate? The manufacturer of the product had even sent her a case of the stuff after the clip went viral.

But Natalie didn't think Alice was the right one to woo wealthy donors into parting with their money at a fancy party.

Before Liam could lob at her any more reasons she shouldn't go, Natalie added, "And the nice ghosts from the Stanley Theater will all be there with me."

"Oh, great. I'm sure they'll be very helpful. And maybe the ghosts from the old New York State Lunatic Asylum, also conveniently located in Utica, will hear about it and join you too. That should be fun. You can have a big old ghost gathering."

Liam scowled while Natalie tried not to be impressed at the level of digging Liam had done just to boss her around. She'd done a little research herself. That asylum he'd mentioned had opened in the eighteen hundreds and closed in the nineteen seventies.

"What's the big guy bitching about now?"

Natalie startled at the male voice behind her. She spun to see Gabe standing just inside the window he'd silently slipped through.

"He doesn't want me to go to Utica," she explained to the ghost, then heard the huff from Liam.

"I take it somebody is in here with us," Liam grumbled.

"Yes. It's Gabe," she answered.

"Good. Maybe you'll listen to Gabe when he tells

you not to go since you won't listen to me. He was there for the supposedly *not* demonic presence." Liam pursed his lips in what would definitely be considered a pout on a less manly man.

"He's so funny when he's jealous." Gabe chuckled, enjoying Liam's displeasure too much, as usual.

"Stop," she warned her ghost best friend low.

Gabe rolled his eyes. "Fine. No more teasing the big guy. But *that's* what he's worried about? Harriet got rid of that spirit. He's gone"

Natalie nodded to Gabe. "Exactly."

"Of course, that doesn't mean there aren't others," Gabe said. "In fact, there probably are more dark entities given the history of some of those buildings. Harriet told us all about it. Liam's right. It doesn't hurt to be careful."

Natalie scowled. She hated when the two men in her life—or rather one man and one ghost—ganged up against her.

"But if Liam's so worried, why doesn't he just go with you?" Gabe asked.

She shook her head. "Can't."

"Why not? He doesn't punch a time clock. He runs a cadaver lab, for God's sake. His test subjects have nowhere else to be since they're—you know— dead. He can't leave to go with you for one day?"

"Nope."

"Why not? Has he got an appointment? A scheduling conflict?" Gabe let out a snort.

Natalie lifted one shoulder. "Actually, yes."

"What, is he having a 'meeting of the minds' with the refrigerator full of brains he's carving up over there?" Gabe chuckled at his own joke.

She laughed along with him. "Maybe."

"As riveting as your half of this one-sided, one-word conversation is, I can't hear your bestie. Would you like to fill me in on the discussion since I have no doubt it's about me?" Liam asked.

Balancing her ghost best friend and her real live boyfriend had proven challenging since she started to see the dead well over a year ago. She would have thought it would have gotten easier by now. It hadn't.

Natalie spun back to Liam. "Gabe says he agrees with me that the problematic spirit moved on after Harriet spoke with it and you have absolutely nothing whatsoever to worry about."

"Gotta love how you relay just the parts you want him to hear and not the rest." Gabe cocked up a brow beneath his ever-present hat.

She ignored Gabe and focused on Liam. "So, see? It's perfectly safe for me to go."

"You know, Nat, if you're lying Gabe does have the

means to relay the truth to me." Though he couldn't see him, Liam glanced over her head in the direction of where Gabe stood. "I can trust you to do that. Right, Gabe?"

Gabe smiled and said, in spite of the fact Liam could not hear him, "Yes you can, big guy."

She narrowed her eyes at the ghost. "Traitor."

Gabe lifted a shoulder. "Come on, Nat. You know what they say. Bros before—"

She raised one finger in warning. "Don't you finish that sentence."

Gabe smiled wider but kept his mouth shut.

It didn't matter. Gabe and Liam could bond all they wanted, but she was going to Utica. Alone. And everything was going to be fine... she hoped.

Chapter Two

"TIME TO HIT THE ROAD"

"I can't believe they didn't invite me to come," Alice Mudd huffed out, arms crossed as she glared at Natalie from the sidewalk outside the shop.

Today the eighty-something-year-old—or possibly ninety-year-old since no one was really sure and everyone was afraid to ask—was dressed in her usual day-to-day outfit. The blindingly white sneakers set off an orange sweatsuit sporting a tropical pattern featuring big pink flowers and bright green leaves.

Florida rest home casual was Alice's signature look even though they lived in upstate New York. Only the colors and patterns of the pants, shirt and zip-up changed. But even today's explosion of color couldn't brighten the dark expression on Alice's face at being snubbed by the event organizers.

"I'm sure it's nothing personal, Alice. It's only because of my—" Natalie stopped mid-sentence.

Because of her what? Whatever this new ability to speak to the dead was, she wasn't sure she could put a name to it. Talent? Skill? Curse? All applied.

Natalie cleared her throat and began again. "It's just because they want me to make a big show for the donors by talking with the ghosts."

"Humph. I remember Harper and I practically had to drag you to Utica to be on the ghost show. Seems like now you don't need me or Harper anymore." Alice's pout had Natalie glancing down guiltily at the car keys in her hand.

"You could come with me as my plus one, if you wanted..." The moment the words were out of her mouth, Natalie regretted them.

"Whoop! I thought you'd never ask." Her steps short but quick, Alice hustled to the corner of the old train depot that Natalie had converted into the book and wine shop. She emerged from the side of the building with a suitcase in her hand. "I'm ready to go."

"You're already packed." It wasn't a question. More a statement of resignation on Natalie's part as Alice dragged her ancient looking suitcase toward the car.

"Yes, I am. So unless you're waiting around to say

goodbye to Doctor McHottie, it's time to hit the road."

"I already said goodbye to Liam."

"I bet you did. *Wink.*" As she said the word, Alice did indeed deliver an exaggerated, open-mouthed wink.

It was the same trademark Alice wink that had also gone viral on social media in various memes made from clips of the show they'd been on. Liam was right. Alice was a bigger star than Natalie. And for better or worse, Alice was going to be at tonight's fundraiser.

It was going to be interesting.

Speaking of the fundraiser... "Alice, tonight's event is fancy. Did you pack something dressy to wear?"

The suitcase Alice had brought for their one-night visit was big enough to hold half of Alice's wardrobe, but Natalie had a suspicion it could very well be filled with nothing more than a rainbow of sweatsuits and a month's supply of Gas-X.

"Oh, sure." Alice nodded. "I always carry something dressy with me. You never know when you'll get invited someplace classy and need it."

Natalie cringed as she considered what Alice considered dressy and classy. "Um, it's not a bedazzled sweat suit, is it?"

"No, but I do have one of those for tomorrow."

When Alice didn't elaborate on what tonight's outfit actually was, Natalie drew in a breath and let it out on a sigh. "Okay."

With that, she let the subject drop and started the car's engine. She wasn't the fashion police. It wasn't her responsibility to dress Alice for the fundraiser.

"Too bad Harp couldn't come," Alice said as she buckled the seat belt.

"Yes, it is," Natalie agreed with a twitch of her lips as she remembered how annoyed Harper would get on set when Alice insisted on calling her 'Harp' for short.

After that short conversational interlude, Alice occupied herself with—surreally—playing silently on her smart phone.

Natalie should have been grateful. An hour and a half of silence had to be better than ninety minutes of making small talk with Alice.

Apparently Natalie wasn't the kind of person to be comfortable with silence in the presence of another person. They made it to the entrance to the highway at the end of town but hadn't even gotten to the sign for the next exit yet when Natalie couldn't take the quiet any longer. "Alice, you can turn on the radio if you want."

"No, thanks," she answered, then set her cell down in her lap and stared out the side window, looking perfectly content to watch miles of nothingness speed by at sixty-five miles per hour.

It was going to be a long, awkward drive.

That thought alone had Natalie trying again to make conversation. "I'm excited to be going back to Utica again. I've only been there twice. Once for the show, then again when Liam and I went back for a visit. But I bet you've been there a lot."

"Not since the DMV took my license away for no good reason, I haven't," Alice answered with a scowl.

Crud. Natalie had broached a touchy subject.

She scrambled to bring the conversation back to safer territory. "But when you were younger, you must have gone there, right?"

"Oh, sure. My older sister Agatha and I used to take the train to Utica."

"The train from Mudville? From, like, the train station that I now own?" Natalie asked, intrigued.

Nowadays only the occasional freight train rumbled by, which was for the best actually. Every train shook the building. It was like living through a mini earthquake every time, multiple times a day until she feared the wine bottles would vibrate off the shelves. The books would survive a fall but the wine wouldn't. For that very reason she made sure no merchandise at *Once Upon a Vine Books & Wine* sat anywhere near the front edge of the display shelves.

"The very same. Back before they shut down the line in 1960, your place was a passenger depot. We'd get on in Mudville, switch trains in New Berlin, then get off in Utica. Agatha and I would have a meal, visit the shops, see a show, then come home."

Surprised, Natalie glanced at Alice. "At the Stanley Theater?" Where they'd spent a week together filming the ghost show, yet Alice had never mentioned even once she'd been there before? Likely many times.

"Sure. Sometimes. And the other theaters too. There was a whole theater district in Utica until they knocked them down in the sixties. Or was it the seventies? Only the Stanley was saved."

Natalie tried to imagine a young Alice and her sister, dressed up to the nines. Out on the town for dinner and a show in a theater district that no longer existed. "Wow. That must have been amazing back then."

"It was." Alice nodded, her voice sounding dreamy, as if she were lost in the past, until she said, "Oops. Sorry. Better crack a window. But don't worry, I packed the Gas-X for later."

Chapter Three

"ALICE IS A STAR"

"Hey, Alice!"

"Alice! Over here."

"Alice, who are you wearing?"

Paparazzi. In Utica. And they were swarming Alice. But she was handling it like a pro, smiling and twirling for them to display a dress that was so old it was back in fashion again.

Tonight was surreal and they'd only just arrived at the train station for the event.

If Natalie were a better person, she'd text Liam and tell him he'd been absolutely correct about Alice's celebrity. That after her memorable participation in the reality show, Alice was no doubt a bigger star than Natalie was.

There were two reasons—at least in her own

mind—Natalie wasn't going to do that. One, Liam didn't need any more fuel for his ego. The *I told you so* gene was strong in that man. And two, Natalie had never disagreed with Liam. She would freely admit Alice had stolen the show quite a few times during that week they'd spent locked in the Stanley Theater with the cast and crew, not to mention the resident ghosts.

Yes, Natalie had the ability to see and hear the dead, but Alice had an innate knack for stealing the scene. But when choosing who would be better at sweet talking potential donors at a fundraising event, Alice was not even in the top ten choices from the show's cast—and there were only eight members in the cast.

"Alice is a star. How are you feeling about that, Nat?"

Natalie spun at the question and smiled when she saw the familiar face.

The costume designer had died in his prime but at least had the good fortune of living out his afterlife in the theater. "Bobby LaRue. I'm so glad you're here. How are you?"

"Well, I'm still dead but otherwise I'm fine. We all are. Of course Evie and Vinny have been driving us all crazy since they got married. Fighting at the top of their lungs one moment, then sneaking off to 'make up' the next, if you catch my meaning."

Natalie laughed. "That sounds about right."

The two dead movie stars from the dawn of the golden age of cinema had had a volatile, sexually charged relationship before they decided they were in love, as well as in lust, with one another. Why would their posthumous marriage change anything?

"The others should be along soon," Bobby said as his gaze dropped down to take in Natalie's outfit. The unspoken critique was clear in his expression.

Natalie sighed. "Go ahead. Say what you have to say about what I'm wearing."

He tipped his head to the side. "Eh. It could be worse. It could also be better."

For a man who was destined to eternally be wearing the same purple leisure suit he died wearing in 1981, he'd always had a lot to say about Natalie's clothes—usually none of it good.

Natalie pulled her mouth to the side. "Thanks."

"Alice, on the other hand, looks fabulous. I'm going to need you to ask her for the story behind how she got an authentic Halston original."

"Is that what it is?" Natalie's gaze shot to Alice, who she had to admit really had come prepared with an appropriate outfit.

"Yes, my little fashion-challenged lumberjack. It is."

She frowned at the insult. "Hey. You don't get to call me that. I'm not wearing my Ugg boots today."

"No, you're not. And thank God for small favors," Bobby said as he glanced down at her black knee-high leather boots. "It's obvious you have a boot fetish but do you own any actual shoes?"

"Yes." She pouted.

"Not clogs. Not sneakers. Not those God-awful croc things." Bobby gave a little shudder. "I mean *real* shoes. I'd settle for just a plain neutral-colored pump with a stiletto heel. Or maybe a peep toe or a sling back."

"I'm sorry to disappoint but to be fair, I'm known for my ability to communicate with you lovely spirits, not for my fashion sense."

"Obviously."

Natalie sighed. Good thing she'd grown a thick skin when it came to ghostly insults. She'd give Bobby a pass. Being dead had to be frustrating. Even so, she glanced down at herself one more time. Her boots were perfectly appropriate. As was her A-line, tea-length, black satin cocktail dress with three-quarter sleeves.

"Looks like Alice has an admirer." Bobby's comment brought Natalie's head up.

She expected to see one of the older male guests. What she saw was a young man, barely twenty years old if she had to guess, dressed in a dirt and blood-stained military uniform. He hung along the edge of the train station's main lobby, his gaze focused solely on Alice. No one else seemed to be looking at him except for Natalie and Bobby. Not even Alice had noticed his intense stare.

"He must be—"

"A ghost? Yes," Bobby supplied.

"What uniform is that?"

"Army. World War II, I'd guess. And might I say that I find it kind of comforting that you're as ignorant about historical fashion as you are contemporary." Bobby's thinly plucked dark brows rose in judgment.

Natalie didn't have time to spar with the designer. She was too intrigued with Alice's admirer.

"I'm going to talk to him," Natalie declared.

Bobby let out a sniff. "And say what?"

"I'll ask him what his interest is in Alice. I mean, he might have technically been in existence for a hundred years, but he's got a body that looks like he's too young to legally order a drink at the bar and he's ogling a woman old enough to be his great grandmother. There's got to be a story there."

"And you're just going to march over and demand to know what it is?" Bobby asked, eyes wide.

"Not demand. Just ask nicely."

"*Ask nicely*, she says." Bobby snorted. "Not all spirits are as nice as *moi*. Do you not remember what happened at the Hotel Utica? Because *I* seem to recall Vinny and I having to find you a *priest* to banish that demon before he did permanent damage to you livings."

Et tu, Bobby? Were all the males in the universe psychically connected when it came to harping on her safety?

"You sound like Liam now. It wasn't like your ghost priest performed an exorcism or anything. He and Harriet just spoke with the—"

"Demon entity," Bobby said.

"Disgruntled spirit," Natalie corrected a bit more loudly. "And he left on his own accord."

"If you say so. And speaking of that hunka, hunka burning love of yours, is Liam coming tonight?" Bobby asked, glancing around hopefully.

"No. Alice is my date tonight." And Natalie intended to discover what was up with her date's admirer.

The young soldier had moved closer to Alice now. Within touching distance as Alice juggled a drink, her purse, a napkin and a loaded plate of appetizers. He only had eyes for her and Natalie needed to know why.

There was definitely a story there and she was going to find out what it was before this night was over.

With the curiosity killing her, Natalie took a step in Alice's direction.

"You're going to talk to that soldier, aren't you?" Bobby's question came out sounding like more of a statement.

"Yup." Ignoring the less than subtle judgement in his tone, she said, "You coming?"

"Of course, I am. Don't be silly."

She smiled. Chalk one up for Bobby's love of gossip and a good story. With any luck, Alice's mysterious soldier was going to provide both.

Chapter Four

"LONG LOST LOVE"

"Um, hi. Can I ask you—"

"Holy mother of God." The young soldier pressed a hand to his chest on a gasp. "You can see me?"

"Yes."

"But you're a living," he said still looking baffled.

"Yes, she is," Bobby agreed. "Long story short, she died very briefly and when she woke up she could see and hear us spirits."

"That's... quite a story," the young man said, eyeing Natalie.

"It is. I'm thinking you have quite a story to tell as well. Would you mind if I asked you a few questions?" she began.

"I guess that would be all right. What d'you wanna know?"

"I'm sorry. I should introduce myself first. My name's Natalie. This is Bobby. And you are?"

"Frankie Donovan. Private. Tenth Army infantry division."

"Frankie. You seem to have an interest in my friend Alice."

"*Alice.* So it is her. I thought so. It had to be." He shook his head in amazement. "Alice. Here. After all these years..."

"Um, how do you know Alice?" Natalie asked.

His gaze dropped shyly. "I... we..." Frankie opened and closed his mouth again, apparently at a loss for words.

"Ooo. This is going to be good." Bobby rubbed his hands together. "Come on, kid. Stories are meant to be shared."

Frankie raised his eyes to Bobby, then shifted his gaze to Natalie. "I guess it's okay. It's been so long. It's just, a man doesn't kiss and tell."

"Told you it was going to be good." Bobby elbowed Natalie in the side, but his elbow did nothing but pass through her.

She shivered from the sensation but kept her focus on Frankie. "What happened so long ago, Frankie?"

"It was 1945. Spring and the weather was perfect. I was home here in Utica on leave for a week visiting my family. I was killing time, having an egg cream at the soda counter inside the drugstore when I spotted her. Alice. Though I didn't know her name at first. She was in town with her sister to see a show and she was the most beautiful girl I'd ever seen."

Natalie pressed her hand to her chest at the romance of it all. "So you talked to her."

Frankie laughed. "Yeah, we talked. For hours. Her sister was so mad. They had plans to do things and I guess I got in the way, but I didn't care. I was shipping out with my unit in just a couple of days. We were headed to Japan. I was young but I knew enough to live every second like it was my last. Turns out, it was a good thing I did."

"You were killed," Natalie guessed in barely a whisper.

Expression somber, he nodded. "Battle of Okinawa. We—the dead—were eventually shipped home. My parents buried me here."

"And your spirit stayed tethered to your body." Natalie sighed. "I am sorry."

He lifted one shoulder. "It's not so bad. I got to see my family and friends again—even if they couldn't see me. And now Alice again. After all this time."

He glanced in Alice's direction, then looked back at Natalie.

"I kept her with me though. Then and now." He tipped the combat helmet he'd held clutched by his side so Natalie could see. There, tucked safely inside was a picture of Frankie smiling in a fresh, clean Army uniform, his arm looped through that of a girl who could only be a young Alice.

Fighting tears, Natalie swallowed, then said, "Wow. But I don't understand how you recognized her. 1945 is a long time ago."

He smiled sadly. "Yes, it is. But I've seen her a few times since that first time. After I...passed. She and her sister continued to come to Utica once in a while. It's one reason I started hanging around the train station. Then she stopped coming."

He visibly shook the memories away then focused on Natalie again.

"She's older now, of course. But she's wearing the same ring. The same necklace. And believe it or not, one time she came to the theater, decades ago, she was wearing that very dress."

Natalie shook her head. "That's incredible."

"See. Take note. That's the power of fashion," Bobby whispered.

"Shush," Natalie reprimanded him, then turned to Frankie. "Do you want to talk to her? I could relay to her whatever you wanted to say."

His eyes widened. They were pale blue beneath the shock of curly blond hair that rested on his forehead. He shook his head. "No. I don't think so. But thank you for offering."

"Of course." Natalie nodded, her heart breaking for the young soldier. And for the young Alice in the picture.

He moved as though to leave, then he pivoted back. "Has she had a happy life?"

Natalie delivered a teary smile. "I can honestly say Alice Mudd is the happiest person I know. She lives life to the fullest. I can only hope to do as well myself."

"Good. Good." He tipped his head to Natalie, then he moved away through the crowd. Although Natalie had a feeling he'd be somewhere nearby watching for the rest of the night, lost in his memories.

"Oh my God, Bobby," Natalie squeaked past the lump in her throat.

"I know. Rip my heart out, why don't you," he agreed.

"I have to say something to Alice."

"Do you though?" Bobby asked. "Soldier boy didn't want to."

"No, but—"

"You're going to anyway," Bobby completed Natalie's thought.

"Hush. I've been given this... ability for some reason. Maybe this is it. Maybe he can move on if I talk to Alice. Perhaps this is his unfinished business."

"His what?" Bobby choked. "You don't still buy into that theory, do you? That we only hang around if we have unfinished business? If that were true, Evie and Vinny would have moved on when you solved their murder."

"*But* they were in love and didn't want to move on." Done debating ghost theories with Bobby, Natalie said, "I'm talking to her. You don't have to come if you don't approve."

"Hell if I'm not coming. Approve or not, this is the most exciting thing to happen around here since the first time you stepped foot in Utica. I'm not missing it."

With Bobby in tow, Natalie moved across the room to where Alice had moved on to perusing the table of bite-sized sweets laid out for the guests.

"Alice."

"Nat. You missed it. They had tiny cannoli." She leaned in conspiratorially. "But don't worry. I put a bunch in my purse for later."

"Oh. Okay. Thanks." Pushing away the slightly disturbing concept of eating one of Alice's purse cannoli, Natalie said, "Alice. Do you remember coming here with your sister to see a show in the Spring of 1945."

"Of course, I do. I told you about that in the car." Alice frowned. "Are you having memory loss? You should talk to Doc Hottie about that."

"No. I'm fine. Do you remember meeting a handsome young soldier on that trip?"

The question had Alice pausing just a beat and looking at Natalie a bit strangely. "Yes."

"Frankie Donovan?" Natalie prompted.

Alice nodded. "I was fifteen. He was going to turn eighteen that summer. He was shipping out in a couple of days with his unit. We spent most of the day together. He walked us to the train that night and before we boarded, he kissed me goodbye. It was my first real kiss. I gave him my address so we could write but he never did."

Throat tight, Natalie said, "He never wrote because he couldn't. He was...killed in battle."

"He—his ghost—was here? You talked to him?"

"I did. Then he left."

Alice nodded again, slowly. "I think I need to visit the ladies room."

As Alice moved away, Natalie lost her battle to control her tears. She spun to face Bobby.

"Oh my God. This is the saddest story I've ever heard," she whispered.

"I know. Right?" Bobby agreed with a sniff.

"Natalie!"

She turned at the sound of her name. The sight of Liam standing there and looking amazing in a tuxedo made her weak in the knees.

Swiping the tears away, she asked, "Liam, what are you doing here?"

He gripped both her shoulders and pinned her with his gaze. "I finished my meeting early so I came to be with you. But what's wrong? What happened? Why are you crying?"

"I'm crying too. You can comfort me," Bobby said with a lascivious look in his tear-filled eyes while standing too closely to Liam for Natalie's liking.

"I'm fine. It's just Alice..." Natalie began as Liam wrapped his arms more tightly around her.

It felt so good to have him there with her. Have him holding her like he was never letting go. After hearing Alice and Frankie's story, she'd never take for granted ever again the fact she was blessed enough to have Liam in her life, every day, safe.

He pulled back again, eyes wide. "Oh, no. Natalie, what happened to Alice?" Liam's tone dipped low as he said, "Is she... she's not..."

Realization hit. "Oh, God. No, Liam. She's not *dead*," Natalie whispered the last word.

"Then what's wrong?" he asked, rubbing those big warm hands up and down her arms.

Natalie was having trouble concentrating. Liam looked damn good in a tux. "Do you own that?" she asked, fingering his lapel.

He frowned then realized she was asking about the tuxedo. "Yeah. I was in a buddy's wedding a few years back. It was easier to just buy one rather than rent-- Why are we talking about my clothes? What happened to Alice?"

"I will admit, he cleans up nice. Not that I wouldn't like him dirty too..." Bobby licked his lips.

Forcing her mind off the ghost ogling her boyfriend and back to Liam's question, Natalie said, "I just found out something really sad about her past and I had to tell her but I'm not sure how she's dealing with it. She excused herself to the ladies room but I think she might be upset."

"What did you find out?" he asked.

Natalie repeated the heart-wrenching story to Liam, tearing up again during the telling.

She let out her breath in a huff when she'd finished relaying the tale. "I don't know. Was I wrong? Maybe I shouldn't have told her. Dammit. I hate this. I wish I never got this stupid power to be able to talk to ghosts."

"Hey, Nat—"

Natalie spun to face the woman. "Alice, you're back."

"Of course, I'm back. Where would I go? You drove me here." After a cock of her brow that clearly said, *duh,* Alice turned to Liam. "Hello, Liam. Hubba-hubba. You're looking good."

Liam smiled. "Thanks, Alice. So are you."

Meanwhile, Natalie was trying to decide if Alice was really good at hiding her emotions or if she just had no heart because Natalie and Bobby seemed much more affected by Frankie's story than Alice did.

"Thanks, doc. Nat, the head guy of this shindig asked if you'd be starting your ghost tour soon." Alice hooked a thumb in the direction from which she'd come.

The tour completely forgotten until now, Natalie wasn't going anywhere until she knew Alice was okay. "Alice, are you all right?"

"Sure. Why wouldn't I be?"

"I just... I mean Frankie... He was..."

"Her long lost love? The one who got away? A love that traverses time and the veil between the living and the dead?" Bobby supplied not so helpfully.

Natalie did her best to ignore the ghost chatter only she could hear. "I just thought you might be sad. That he died."

"Natalie, everybody dies eventually," Alice said matter-of-factly.

"You're right. Of course. I just thought you might be sad for... what could have been."

"Natalie, if I'd dated Frankie back then, if he'd made it home and we got married, my life would have turned out completely different. I doubt I would have gone to college. I wouldn't have had a career teaching. Instead of Mudville, we would have lived here in Utica where he had a job waiting in the family business." Alice shook her head. "No. I like my life the way it was. The way it is now. I'm happy and a person can't be happy if they have regrets."

"Wise words, Alice," Liam said as he squeezed Natalie's waist with one big warm hand. "You should listen to her, babe."

Subtlety wasn't Liam's forte. That comment was no doubt in response to her saying she wished she never got the ability to talk to the dead and that she regretted telling Alice about Frankie.

"I do have one question though," Alice began. "Wait. Two actually."

"Of course. Anything." Natalie nodded as she tried

to remember every word Frankie had said so she could relay them to Alice.

"One, is Doc Hottie sharing our hotel room tonight and two, does he sleep in the nude?" Alice asked.

"Both excellent inquiries," Bobby said. "I'd like to know the answers as well."

Surprised once again by Alice Mudd, Natalie couldn't help but smile.

This was her life now, strange though it was, and just like Alice, Natalie knew deep down that she wouldn't want it any other way.

The Graveyard Secrets Series

CADAVER LAB: A ROMANTIC COMEDY

CADAVER LAB 2: GHOSTLY HEARTS & BODY PARTS

CADAVER LAB 3: SPIRITED SHENANIGANS

CADAVER LAB 4: GRAVE'S ANATOMY

A top 10 *New York Times* and nine-time *USA Today* bestselling contemporary romance author, Cat Johnson writes hot alpha heroes (who often wear cowboy or combat boots) and the sassy heroines brave enough to love them.

Known for her creative marketing, Cat has sponsored bull riding cowboys, promoted romance using bologna and owns a collection of cowboy boots and camouflage for book signings.

She writes full time from a Queen Anne Victorian in a small town in upstate New York suspiciously like Mudville where she tends to her backyard chickens and too many cats. Learn more at catjohnson.net.

Get book news and subscriber exclusives. Join the newsletter list at catjohnson.net/news or scan the code.

WELCOME TO
Mudville
NEW YORK
Bethany's House
Cadaver Lab
STATION
Honey Buns
Library
Agnes's House
Once Upon a Time Books & Wine
Variety Store
Main Street
DINER
BURGERS MALTS
Red's Shop
RIP
Mudville House
Mudville Diner
Rose's
Muddy River
Muddy River Inn
Morgan Farm Market
"Mudville" by Cat Johnson inspired by Unadilla, NY

www.ingramcontent.com/pod-product-compliance
Lightning Source LLC
Chambersburg PA
CBHW051412130726
47987CB00007B/2964